Wild Horses
for
Wild Kids

Stu Campbell

ISBN: 978-0-9962019-6-4

6   5   4   3   2   1

Edited by Mira Perrizo
Cover and text design by D.K. Luraas
Cover painting by Larry Jones, Bouse, Arizona

Printed in the United States of America

Contents

Career Choices

Some years had passed since Jimmy McIntyre had left the Wilson Ranch. He'd graduated from high school and even went on to college, continuing to work for Honey at the ranch during the summers. He'd developed his cowboy skills to the point where he'd make a good hand on any outfit, although he'd never become a top-notch bronc rider, but his roping had improved to the point where he felt fairly confident about his ability to catch something when he threw a loop at it.

Jimmy had majored in criminology in college, mostly at the urging of Bill Mason, his probation officer from his earlier years. Jimmy and Mason had become good friends over the years. He was on probation when Bud Wilson gave him a job on the ranch, mostly because Bud knew Jimmy's parents and thought Jimmy had just fallen in with the wrong crowd and needed an even chance. With Bill Mason's approval and approval from the juvenile court judge, he went to work on the ranch. He was guaranteed a job every summer if he stayed in high school and as long as his grades and his job performance were acceptable.

"You've proven yourself on the ranch, you can do anything you want with a college education," said Mister Mason during one of their earlier conversations.

"But I've studied all through high school, and I'm tired of it," said Jimmy. "What would I take up in college?"

"Anything you want to. You could even go into criminology," replied Mason.

"Criminology? Why?"

"You've already been a part of the criminal system," answered Bill Mason. "You're familiar with it, its shortcomings and its positive aspects."

"I am? What do you mean?"

Mason replied, "Aren't you aware that when you went to work for the Wilsons, you started to make some positive changes in your life? The judge that allowed you to work out on that ranch told me that if you didn't change your ways you'd end up spending a good part of your life, perhaps all of it, in the prison system. He also told me that he'd probably be the one to incarcerate you and he didn't look forward to doing that."

"I'm aware of that," replied Jimmy, "but it was my understanding that Mister Wilson needed some help."

"Bud Wilson did need help. But you actually needed him more than he needed you. He gave you an even chance to learn how to work, accept responsibility, and become a worthwhile member of society. It was a great idea he had and he had to go to the judge and get his permission then come to me and get my okay. The deal has worked so well that I've had some ideas about creating a kids' camp for these juvenile delinquents in the hope of improving their chances in life. You're the proof. You turned out better than I expected ..."

"Because I'm black?" asked Jimmy.

"No," answered Mason, smiling. He had the thought that it would be a while before Jimmy considered himself as another member of society and not another black member of society. Society itself was largely responsible for that and perhaps that would change in time.

"Because of your previous record," continued Mason. "Look at you now. You've graduated from high school and you weren't even in school when Bud hired you. You have the whole world ahead of you and it's up to you to make the most of it. You can make the most of yourself and perhaps even positively influence someone else."

"I can do that?" asked Jimmy.

"Certainly! I've been so impressed with you that I even tried to convince Bud Wilson to turn his ranch into a juvenile detention rehabilitation center for teenagers."

"He wouldn't go for that," replied Jimmy.

"I knew that, but I tried anyway. However, he did make some helpful suggestions. And I've been working on them in my spare time. At any rate, if you were to go into criminology, you could be most helpful in helping me to achieve my goals in helping others."

"How could I help you?"

"I'm thinking that perhaps we could use you as a positive example of the improvements we need to make in the juvenile detention program. It would mean making public your previous criminal record, the fact that you weren't in school and that you were involved in some unacceptable actions. Then we would explain in detail your experiences, both good and bad, at the Wilson Ranch and look to your graduating from high school as a direct result of positive action on your part and the part of the courts. If you were in college, we could point out that your being there is a direct result of this change in the way the courts are handling the juvenile delinquent problem."

"But if I majored in criminology in college, what would I do if I graduated?"

If I graduated, thought Mason. *There's still an element of self-doubt in Mister McIntyre.*

Undaunted, Mason replied, "You could become a probation officer like I am, a parole officer, or any other numerous occupations in that field." Mason wondered if the reference to his position might influence Jimmy negatively. Mason didn't really figure himself above and beyond others. He just had a job to do and was trying to do his best at it.

"But, I've come to like ranch life," said Jimmy. "I don't think I'd want to get too far away from it."

"Here's why I want you," said Mason. "This is the beauty of the situation. You've had experience in the juvenile court system and on a working dude ranch. On the ranch, you've had to deal with horses, cattle, and people. My plan is to incorporate potential juvenile delinquents, cattle, and horses into a rehabilitation program that really works. It's worked well with you, you're the proof.

"I know we can't use the Wilson Ranch. But if we can find a similar ranch and acquire it, we can begin a test program. We would need to convince the state legislature that such a program would benefit those individuals that needed it and would benefit society as a whole. And we would need to convince them well enough that they would allocate funding for the project.

"That's where you come in. As I said, you're the proof. If we can convince the state legislature that the idea works, I would want you to manage the ranch. This is not a guarantee, but I would want you involved in the program, if we can get it going. You would be the example."

"I don't know that I can be an example to anybody," replied Jimmy.

"Ah," said Mason, "the nice part is that you don't have to try to be an example. Just be what you are, be yourself, that's enough of an example. What do you think of the idea so far?"

"I like the idea of being a ranch manager," replied Jimmy. "But I don't think I could be as good a manager as Bud Wilson or Honey."

"Well, Bud Wilson's already consented to being a consultant on this program. And even though I haven't talked to Honey about it, I'm sure he wouldn't mind helping out. Are you interested?"

"I am," answered Jimmy, "but I'd like to talk to Bud and Honey before I make a decision."

"That's fair enough," answered Mason. "I understand you've got a job with them if you want it during the summers if you go to college."

"That's right."

On the Wilson Ranch during the summer, Jimmy discussed with Bud Wilson the plan Mister Mason had laid out.

"I think it's a good plan," said Bud, "but have you thought about what college you want to go to and have you made an application?"

"No," replied Jimmy, "but I did go to the state university and looked it over. It appeared okay."

"Well, it doesn't matter what college you go to. Just do a good job if you go. Don't select any field for a major until your second year, that way you can get all the required subjects out of the way and you will be better prepared to make a choice of what field you want to study."

Later that summer, Jimmy received a letter from his mother stating that he'd been accepted at the state university.

"Where did this come from?" asked Jimmy, as he showed the letter to Bud Wilson.

"When you indicated an interest in going to college, I got a hold of your mother and she filled out your application and mailed it to the university."

"Well," said Jimmy, "it looks like I'm going to college."

"Good for you!" said Bud.

During his second year, Jimmy decided to major in animal science and minor in criminology. His college advisor questioned his choices, indicating that most students selected a minor that was closely related to their major field of study.

Jimmy just replied to his advisor's questions with, "It's not a good idea to put all your eggs in one basket."

When Jimmy indicated his fields of study to Bill Mason, Mason seemed to approve, but asked, "Why animal science before criminology?"

Jimmy replied as he had to his college advisor, "It's not a good idea to put all your eggs in one basket." Then he added, "I'm not sure I'm completely sold on your idea yet. And I do know that I don't want to be a cop."

Bud Wilson had provided some financial help for Jimmy and along with his monthly wages he managed to graduate from college. His grades in college were passable, but not outstanding. So, Jimmy McIntyre graduated—wearing cowboy boots and blue jeans under his cap and gown.

Financing

Bill Mason had been working hard on his idea of a juvenile delinquent rehabilitation ranch while Jimmy was in college. In late April during his junior year, Jimmy was asked by Mason to appear before the state legislature and answer questions about his background and his experience as a hired hand on the Wilson Ranch.

When he showed up at the state Capitol, he was pleasantly surprised to see Bud Wilson and Honey there. He'd been out to the ranch to help during the Christmas break, but hadn't had any news since then. He heartedly shook hands with both of them and was filled in with the latest news about the ranch.

Ginny, Honey and Sally's oldest child, was becoming quite the hand on horseback. Honey had bought her a Welsh pony, and she insisted on saddling it herself every time she used it.

"The girl's growin' like a weed," said Honey. "I suspect she'll be as good a hand as her mother. She'd rather be out helpin' with the cattle than doin' the pony walks with Einstein! She's in school, of course, an' Sally an' Ginny an' Chet have been in town all winter except for the Christmas break."

A year or so before, Sally and Honey had another child, a boy. They named him Chester after Bud's father, but they call him Chet. "He's talkin' an' he ain't walkin', he's runnin'. He's 'bout run me ragged."

Honey went on to fill in Jimmy on how Sally, Missus Abercrombie, the cook, Pat, and everyone, including the livestock, were doing.

"I understand we've got to testify before the legislature," said Bud Wilson.

Jimmy's parents showed up for the hearing. His mother said, "We wanted to be here for this. Not one member of our family has ever been asked to testify before the state legislature. This is an honor for our family."

"Not before the state legislature," said Mason, as he approached with the judge that had approved Jimmy's working at the Wilson's. "This is a subcommittee that will, if we are successful, recommend our ideas to the whole legislature in the form of a bill, and if passed, to the governor for his signature. I know one of the men on the committee and we have a good chance of being successful. If we're successful, we can start looking for property any time. We need to get pictures of all of us so I've brought a photographer along. He's from the newspaper—we'll need all the favorable publicity we can get."

Bud Wilson, Honey, the judge, Bill Mason, and Jimmy posed for pictures. Mason hoped they would help if a newspaper article was written about his cause.

The hearing began with Mason stating his purpose in being there: "To obtain the support of the government and funds sufficient to obtain a ranch where juvenile delinquent youngsters could have an opportunity to learn responsibility and be better prepared to reenter society as a productive individual rather than an individual just released from reform school." He stated Jimmy's history of juvenile delinquency, his experience at the Wilson Ranch, and concluded by saying, "The young man I have described is present today and willing to make known his experiences to you."

Mason also made a request for money to be made available to fund the project.

"That's fine," said the senator chairing the committee, "but I think the committee would like to hear from the honorable Judge Reynolds. What is your opinion regarding this matter, Judge?"

The judge stood up and began, "Honored Chairman, senators, and guests, it is a genuine pleasure to address this hearing on behalf of a program Mister Mason has suggested which, if success-ful, could drastically revamp and improve the methods we presently use in treating juvenile offenders. As a judge involved in the juvenile court system and having heard many cases involving juvenile of-fenders over the years, I find it personally and professionally dis-tressing to sentence many of these youngsters, who are obviously bright and intelligent individuals, to reform school, knowing that they will not emerge reformed. Chances are, under our present sys-tem of reform, they will emerge better equipped to continue a life of crime."

As the judge continued, Jimmy whispered to Mason, "Is he up for reelection? This sounds like a campaign speech."

"Quiet!" admonished Mason in a harsh whisper. "The judge knows what he's doing."

The judge continued, not hearing Jimmy's comment, "Many of these youngsters just need an honest shot at life. Many come from underprivileged households and many are from single parent households. Quite often, the parents of these youngsters are un-employed or are affected by chronic alcoholism. Many youngsters would become useful members of society if they had an honest opportunity. Our present juvenile system does not allow for oppor-tunity, only what the courts consider a just punishment.

"I am familiar with the youngster Mister Mason referred to, Jimmy McIntyre, having seen him in my court on numerous occa-sions. When Mister Mason and Bud Wilson, a man whom I thor-oughly respect and who is well known for his humanitarian efforts in our county, when they came to me with this idea, I thought it preposterous at the time. But on deeper reflection, I thought it might be worth a try. I remember thinking that at least it would keep Jimmy McIntyre out of my overcrowded court for a while. The program with Jimmy McIntyre has been successful, as Mister McIntyre has not appeared in my court since."

Jimmy smiled at the judge's comment about keeping him out of his court. He really hadn't looked forward to going to court when he had to.

"As a matter of fact," said the judge, "Mister McIntyre has often come to my chambers just to say hello since working at the Wilson Ranch. A pleasant surprise considering that most juvenile offenders want nothing to do with their sentencing judge. During the time spent on the Wilson Ranch, Mister McIntyre not only learned responsibility and how to work, but he learned kindness and courteousness, attributes that our penal system fails to teach these juvenile delinquents.

"In conclusion, I would strongly recommend that this committee listen carefully to Mister McIntyre's story and approve the proposal Mister Mason has suggested. I thank you senators for taking the time to hear this proposal and those people who are here to support it. Thank You."

The judge had ended his speech and as he sat down, the chairman of the committee said, "Thank you for your time. I think now the committee would like to hear from Mister Wilson."

"Thank you, sir," said Bud, as he wheeled himself beside the podium from which the judge had spoken. "I would stand up, but as you can see, I'm somewhat limited."

"That's all right, Bud, er, Mister Wilson," said the chairman.

Jimmy was surprised, he had no idea Bud Wilson knew the chairman.

"I approached Mister Mason about using Jimmy out on our ranch because I knew he was on probation and I knew his parents and I knew Jimmy was headed in the wrong direction by dropping out of school and hanging out with the wrong individuals. I thought Jimmy had more potential and wanted to help out. Mister Mason agreed to my using Jimmy on the ranch and with the court's permission, he came to work for us."

The chairman asked, "How did that work out?"

"Jimmy was mighty green when he came to us, never having had any ranch experience. We had to show him how to do just about everything."

Jimmy grinned when he heard Bud say that, remembering his early days on the ranch.

"But once he learned something," continued Bud, "we left him alone to do his job. It was a rocky beginning, but …"

"You mean you left one of these juvenile delinquents alone?" asked a member of the committee.

"Well," said Bud, "he wasn't exactly alone. My son-in-law, Honey here, supervised him." Bud pointed to Honey as he made this statement. "Honey is our ranch manager and now actually is the ranch owner, along with my daughter. I only reside there during the summer and act as a consultant. But, back to Jimmy, he did his work well and I indicated to him that he had a job the following summer if he went back to school and kept his grades up. He reentered high school and has worked on the ranch every summer since. He graduated from high school and he is presently enrolled ..."

"You mean he was bribed into going back to school," interrupted a senator.

"Not bribed, sir! He was given an incentive!" Bud was annoyed by this view and showed it. But he held his anger and continued, "Jimmy is currently enrolled at the state university and majoring in animal science. Because of Mister Mason's influence he has minored in criminology. He should graduate in June of next year. He has applied himself in every aspect of his life since coming to the ranch."

"Are you leading us to believe every juvenile delinquent that becomes involved in such a program as has been recommended will succeed in all aspects of his life?" The question was asked by the same senator that interrupted Bud earlier. It seemed that this senator was not in favor of the idea and was antagonistic toward it.

"Not every youngster, sir. The individuals placed in such a program should be screened and those individuals showing an inclination to retain an antisocial attitude should not be entered into the program. Of course those individuals showing an honest desire to change should be allowed to enter it. I would suggest that this committee recommend to the legislature that funds be allocated to try this program. We must try to improve these juvenile delinquents' lot in life. Are there any other questions?"

It was obvious Bud was beginning to tire of the proceedings.

The chairman looked at the other members of the committee and not seeing any other questions, said, "We thank you Mister

Wilson. I think the committee would like to hear from the man called Honey."

Honey walked to the podium.

"How did you come by the name 'Honey'"?

"I sure wasn't given it at birth," said Honey. The response brought a laugh from the committee members. Honey related how his wife had given him the nickname and it had stuck, despite his efforts to abandon it.

"What do you know about Jimmy McIntyre?"

"I do know that he was on probation when he came to work for us," replied Honey. "I don't know what he was on probation for or the nature of his previous offenses. But I do know that he had a lot to learn an' he learned it well. In the period of time he worked for us, he became a valued member of our staff and a good friend. He …"

"Was he ever left alone?" The antagonistic senator was good at interrupting.

"Yes he was," answered Honey.

"You mean you left this juvenile delinquent alone on the ranch? How could you do such a thing?"

"That's right. Where was he gonna go? It's about a hundred miles or so to town. Besides that we're runnin' a ranch, not a jail."

"Didn't you think he could hitchhike into town?"

"He'd have had to walk twenty or twenty-five miles to the high-way just to hitchhike," answered Honey. "I didn't think there was much of a chance he'd do that."

"Did you keep a close eye on him?"

"No, I'd give him a job and leave him alone to do it," replied Honey.

"You'd leave him alone? You didn't keep him under constant supervision?"

"Yes, I'd leave him alone and no, I didn't keep him under constant supervision. I was not his probation officer, although I did call Bill Mason once a week with a report on Jimmy," answered Honey.

"Why?"

"Those were the terms of our agreement."

The committee member asked, "Why didn't you keep him under constant supervision?"

"When a person is given a job to do, it's best to leave him alone to do it. All too often, if he's supervised, the supervisor ends up helpin' or doin' the job. It's human nature to want to help. So, Jimmy was left alone and if he needed help, he was told to ask for it. Besides that, I had other chores to do. When an individual completes chores assigned to him, quite often the completion of the chore helps to raise that person's self-esteem. I felt Jimmy could use a boost in that area.

"Now, gentlemen, I feel that this line of questionin' is not really appropriate. We're here to achieve approval of Mister Mason's plan. I have listened carefully to the proceedin's an' I feel like Jimmy is on trial. He actually hasn't done anything wrong; in fact he has turned his life around and is on the right track."

"Thank you Mister Honey," said the chairman. "I think the committee would now like to hear from this Jimmy McIntyre."

Jimmy stood at the podium and told his story in detail. The members of the committee listened courteously and the antagonistic senator didn't interrupt. When Jimmy was done, he finished by saying, "I'd be glad to answer any questions the committee might have."

One of the committee members asked, "Is it my understanding that you didn't come from a broken home or single parent environment?"

"That's correct, sir. It's not a requirement that a person come from a single parent home or broken home to become a juvenile delinquent," replied Jimmy.

The committee members laughed at Jimmy's comment. Jimmy continued, "My parents are here today." Remembering what his mother had said, he added, "My mother said it was an honor to appear before the legislature to promote such a worthy cause."

"That's fine," said the chairman. "If there are no other questions or comments, we can declare these proceedings closed."

Jimmy said, "Before we leave, I'd like to take this opportunity to thank the committee on behalf of Mister Mason, Judge Reynolds, Bud Wilson, Honey, and myself for the opportunity to make our case public and known. Thank you!"

"And the committee thanks all the participants in these proceedings," said the chairman. "These proceedings are officially closed."

The chairman and other members of the committee rose to leave the room. Everyone else remained seated until they left the room.

"I would like to suggest that we all go to lunch," said Mason. "Dutch treat, of course. And please join us, Mister and Missus McIntyre."

A restaurant was selected and half an hour later the group was seated and ordering lunch. After everyone had ordered, Mason said, "I think our hearing before the senators went well. All we can do now is wait."

Jimmy asked, "What will happen while we're waiting?"

"If we have been successful with the committee, they will draw up a bill and present it to the senate. If it passes the senate it will be passed to the house and if it passes the house, it will be presented to the governor for his signature. When he signs it, the bill will become law and we'll be in business. I just hope we requested enough money."

The meal was delivered and the proceedings were discussed while they ate. When dessert was brought, the discussion continued.

"Honey," said the judge, "I think you made a nice presentation. I particularly like the reference to 'Jimmy not being on trial.' That was a big boost."

Honey nodded his head in agreement, having just filled his mouth with a big piece of apple pie and not able to respond verbally.

When the meal was finished, everyone went their separate ways. Before Bud and Honey left for the ranch, Jimmy's mother said, "Here Bud, I have something for you." At the McIntyre's car, Missus McIntyre gave Honey two boxes of jams and jellies and Honey put them in his company car.

"Jams and jellies! We can't hardly keep them in stock from you!" Bud reached for his wallet and pulled out a roll of bills and handed some to Missus McIntyre without counting it. "I hope you're going to keep the ranch stocked with these again this summer."

"I intended to," replied Missus McIntyre. "But I can't take this money for them; you've done so much for Jimmy."

"Well, Jimmy has done a lot for us," said Bud. "Besides, our agreement was that I pay for the jams and jellies. You count that and if there's more than what's due, apply it to the next delivery."

Disappointment then Surprise

A day after the hearing there was an item in the newspaper regarding the hearing. Mason called everyone involved to tell them of the writeup. The article was three columns long and each column was about two-thirds the length of the page. It was accompanied with the picture that had been taken before the hearing.

Mason called Jimmy last. He said, "We made the paper! But we didn't make the front page. You were quoted quite extensively. It looks like we're well on the way. I have high hopes for this program and intend to follow it in person all the way to the end."

Jimmy just said, "Good! Keep me posted." He was involved in school fairly heavily.

A few months later, Jimmy went back to work at the Wilson Ranch. Thoughts of the juvenile delinquent rehabilitation program were not on his mind as he did his work with the dudes, horses, and cattle on the ranch.

One afternoon, Bud Wilson got a call from Bill Mason. "Our plan has failed with the legislature," Mason told Bud. "The house said, 'success of our program with one individual does not guarantee success for many and funds are not available for such a project,' so a bill was not drawn up for the governor's signature. I'd appreciate it if you'd have Jimmy give me a call at my home this evening. I'll break the news to him myself."

"I'll have Jimmy call you after supper," said Bud. They visited a while, Bud got Mason's home phone number and ended the call.

After supper, Bud called Jimmy aside and said, "Call Mister Mason at this number. He sounded down a little, you might help cheer him up." Bud handed Jimmy the paper he'd written Mason's number on."

"What's up?" asked Jimmy.

"I'll let Mister Mason tell you," replied Bud. "Take all the time you need."

Jimmy called Mason and they talked for a long time. When they got done, Bud asked Jimmy, "What's Bill going to do now?"

"He told me there was a lot of support for the program in the legislature," said Jimmy. "The bill was voted down by only a few votes. He says he'll continue to push for approval in his spare time. He said he's spent so much time on this he's fallen behind in his other work."

"He's a fighter," said Bud. "He'll stay on top of this as long as there's a chance, even a small one, of getting state approval."

"There's nothing I can do to help him out now," said Jimmy. "I guess I'll go to bed so I can do something productive here tomorrow."

"Good idea," replied Bud.

The attitude at the Wilson Ranch didn't change because of the failure of Bill Mason's idea with the legislature, but it did change in Mason's office. There was a general feeling of doom and gloom in his office and it was reflected by the entire staff. Noting the dismay that appeared to be shared by his small staff, he said: "Cheer up, the fight is not over. We've just lost the first round, but we've got many to go. This may have been just a pipe dream on my part anyway, so don't let it bother you."

A week after the failure of the bill, Mason got a letter from a Missus Grundy at the far end of the state. The letter, written in firm, graceful longhand stated:

Dear Mr. Mason,

I have followed, in the newspaper, with interest, your cause for a Juvenile Detention Center. I personally feel that such a facility is warranted and needed in the state. I was very much dismayed to see that the state legislature turned down your request. My own son went afoul of the law and consequently is serving time in the state prison system.

The letter went on to explain her son's plight and his experiences in juvenile court and later in criminal court and in prison. Her letter concluded with:

I have a small ranch and am too old to operate it. My son will not be released from prison in the near future. The ranch has a few cows on it and it is only a hundred or so acres. It has a rundown barn, water rights, and a house. The fences need repair. Could I donate this property to you and be assured it would be used to create a juvenile detention facility to give many of these youngsters a fair shot? If such a facility had been available, perhaps my son would not be doing time in the state prison now.

The letter had a phone number and address where Missus Grundy could be reached.

Mason immediately contacted Missus Grundy and made arrangements to meet with her and inspect the property. He took a few days off work and drove to the far end of the state. On the way, he pictured a facility as he'd seen at the Wilson Ranch—well maintained, neat outbuildings, and green grass growing in front of the lodge.

He met Missus Grundy at her residence in town. At first glance he determined that she had seen better years. Her face was deeply wrinkled and showed signs of having been outside in the sun and wind a good many years. He thought she might be bitter about her son's prison sentence and therefore bitter about everything. He was surprised to see a kind, gentle look in her eye, despite her rough appearance, and she was not at all bitter toward the world and all those in it.

Mister Mason drove her to the ranch and in their conversation, Mason found her to be witty and charming. She spoke freely of her son and, in her words, "I'll be long dead when he gets out of prison, if he gets out."

"I understand," said Mason, "according to your letter, that you wish to donate your ranch to our cause. If you do that, what can we expect from your son when he gets out?" Mason was already anticipating possible problems that could arise with this phase of his program.

"From my son, you can expect nothing, while he is in prison or when he gets out. His prison time has done him some good. He's truly remorseful about the crimes he committed. He has followed your cause in the newspaper and actually was in favor of this donation when I told him about it. I would tell you that he actually suggested it, but you would probably think this was an action to show him in a favorable light when his parole hearing came up."

Mason laughed. "You're right about that," he said. He also thought that Missus Grundy was sharper in her mind than her appearance and age would lead one to believe.

The drive to the ranch took about forty-five minutes, during which Mason learned as much as he could about the ranch and the Grundys. He made a mental note to look up Missus Grundy's son's record and familiarize himself with it.

When they reached the ranch, they drove up to the house. There were big shade trees in front, which gave in inviting appearance to the place, but the grass was long dead. Mason was disappointed—the place didn't look anything like he'd envisioned it. It did not resemble the Wilson Ranch as he'd imagined. At first glance, the house looked run down and in a state of great disrepair. The house was small and upon entering it, it was evident that it hadn't been lived in for some time. A good layer of dust covered everything and there were cracks in the windows and walls. There were two bedrooms, a bathroom, living room, and kitchen. The sinks in both the kitchen and bathroom showed signs of rust.

Missus Grundy made no excuse for the condition of the house. "As you can see," she said, "the place hasn't been lived in for some time. I haven't lived here since my son went to prison. However, fixing this place up would be a great project for juvenile delinquents. There's enough to do here to keep a lot of kids off the streets, busy for a long time and out of trouble. The water is good, we drilled a well some years ago."

She went to the fuse box in the corner of the kitchen and flipped the switch up. A few lights came on. Then she turned on the water. "We need electricity to run the water pump." The water ran and it was a dirty brown, rusty color.

Mason looked at the water running with a look of disappointment on his face. Missus Grundy saw the look and said, "Do you want a drink?"

Mason hurriedly declined and as he looked at Missus Grundy, he could see she was joking. *The old gal still has a sense of humor,* he thought.

Mason made a complete inspection of the house, checking out every room, closet, and cupboard. There were signs of mice all over and in almost every corner there was a spider web. In one corner of the kitchen the spider web was so big and thick, Mason thought it was a saddle blanket that was hung up and forgotten about.

Upon completing his inspection of the house he walked out the back door onto a porch. The barn was about fifty yards away and it leaned to the east. The corrals were not even usable; a number of poles were either down or missing.

"I'd like to walk through the barn," said Mason.

"Go right ahead," replied Missus Grundy. "I'll wait here until you return. There's about sixty acres of alfalfa planted east of the barn, the rest of the ground is pasture. Check it out." Missus Grundy sat down on an old swing on the porch.

Mason walked down to the barn. It was in a state of disrepair worse than the house. The barn door was open and as he entered, he saw a jackrabbit run out the opposite door, which was missing. He walked around inside and outside the barn and noted everything that needed repair. He saw an old harness hanging in a corner and ran his hand along the various quarter straps and belly bands. The leather was hard and rotten. The hames were rusted, as were the snaffle bits on the bridles. He became quite discouraged. He determined the whole barn, just like the house, needed complete revamping.

After inspecting the barn thoroughly as he did the house, he walked to the alfalfa field and was surprised to see a good healthy stand of hay. It was obvious someone was taking care of the hayfield.

He returned to the house to find Missus Grundy, still seated on the swing, drinking a glass of water. "Do you want a drink? It's clear, cold, and good."

Mason eyed the water she was drinking, noted its condition,

and said "Sure. I came out here to look and I might just as well try it while I'm here."

The water was still running from the tap. "I had to run the water quite a while before it cleared up and could wash two glasses." She filled up a clean glass and handed it to Mason. Apprehensively, he tried it. He was pleasantly surprised.

"What do you think?" asked the old woman.

"There's a lot of work to be done to make anything out of this place," replied Mason.

"Yes, I know that," replied Missus Grundy. "The place is run down. However, you're looking at what needs to be done rather than looking at what it could be when everything is repaired and in working order."

"Perhaps you're right," said Mason. "The hay seems to be doing well, though. Who takes care of that?"

"The neighbor," replied Missus Grundy. "He irrigates and bales it. He also takes care of the few cows I have and in return keeps all the hay."

"Why do you think this would make a good rehabilitation facility?"

"Look at the location," replied Missus Grundy. "It's pretty out here. It's peaceful and quiet. With the proper improvements and some changes it could become a nice kids' camp. The mountains off to the west are scenic, aspen trees and pines. It's National Forest and there are plenty of trails to ride on. We used to ride them quite often."

"You want to donate the entire place to this kids' rehabilitation camp idea?" asked Mason. "Why?"

"Mister Mason, I'm an old woman and I don't have a lot of time left. I'd hoped my son could take this place and make something out of it, like it used to be. But my son ended up in prison and the place has become run down. I would like to leave something good when I pass and not just a son in prison. I would donate this place to your cause with the stipulation that it be used as a rehabilitation center for the next hundred years or so. I would also need a receipt for tax purposes."

Mason thought, *The old girl is sharper than I thought. She must have plenty of money somewhere. It's certain she's not making any money off this place.*

Mason said, "This is the best option we've got so far, but it will take some time to work out all the details. I'll check with the proper people and see if it's feasible."

"That will be fine," said Missus Grundy. She reached in her purse and pulled out a paper and handed it to Mason. "This is a letter of my intent, properly notarized, just to let everyone concerned know that I'm serious about this."

Mason took the letter and read it over. Missus Grundy was serious about this.

"You're better prepared for this than I am," he said, with renewed respect for the old woman. "I see your lawyer's phone number on this. I'll have our lawyers contact him."

On the trip back to town, Missus Grundy outlined how she envisioned the camp to take place. "This is the way I see it. Of course you can do anything you want after the transfer is made," she said.

"It will take a lot of money to make a kids' camp out of it," said Mason. "The legislature didn't approve our original proposal because of either a lack of funds or the acquisition of a ranch would be too expensive. Either way, it boils down to money."

"How much is one youngster's life worth?" queried Missus Grundy.

"Not much according to the response we received from the legislature," answered Mason. Mason was rather discouraged with his plans and the condition of the Grundy ranch.

Missus Grundy, noting Mason's disappointment, offered another suggestion. "We could set up this program as a private concern, a nonprofit enterprise rather than a state operated program. The state is always too slow in beginning their programs; there's too much red tape and the politicians are always trying to take credit for things they don't do just to get reelected. As a private enterprise, we could solicit donations from civic-minded individuals and corporations. We have the ranch; we wouldn't need as much money as we'd need to go out and buy a place, probably only half the amount you've had in mind."

Mason saw the reasoning and good sense behind the old woman's thinking. He also saw how a nonprofit enterprise could be set up and operating faster than a government program. He began to cheer up as he saw his program taking shape on the Grundy ranch.

But he also saw a potential problem developing. He'd noted Missus Grundy's use of the word "we" in putting forth her views. Mason wondered if she was including herself in the program without being invited. He decided he'd better clear the air of the situation before it went any further. He asked: "To what degree would you want to be involved if we went the nonprofit enterprise route?"

"It would be nice to be on the board of directors," she replied. "But I don't really think I'd belong there. I would want to be informed and invited to the meetings of the board of directors. I would attend such meetings as an interested observer, not a voting member of the board. I can see that you're already thinking I'd like to continue to have some control over the ranch. That is not the case."

Mason marveled at the old woman's insight. "Would you agree in writing to relinquish complete control of the property?"

"Certainly," said Missus Grundy with a laugh.

"Even if improvements were made that did not appear satisfactory to you?"

"Of course," replied Missus Grundy. "Just because I'm donating the ranch doesn't mean I still wouldn't have an interest in it. Whatever has to be done to help a youngster straighten out his life is fine with me. I certainly didn't do a good job with my son. You people are expected to know what you're doing."

"Perhaps," replied Mason, "perhaps."

The last half of the ride back to Missus Grundy's home was spent in silence. Mason contemplated the advantages and disadvantages of operating a nonprofit enterprise. By the time they reached the old woman's house, Mason had decided that the nonprofit enterprise would bear some further investigating. Mason walked Missus Grundy to the door.

"The more I think about it the more I'm inclined to like your nonprofit idea. However, it will take more consideration. Our people will be in touch with you and your lawyers. I sincerely thank you for your time and most kind offer."

"And I thank you, Mister Mason. I surely hope we can make a difference, even if it's a small one. Oh, by the way, I'd like to meet this Jimmy, what was his last name, McIntyre?"

"Yes," replied Mason, "McIntyre is correct. I suppose if this deal goes through, I'll be out here quite often. I will bring him on the next trip I make."

"Fine, fine," replied Missus Grundy. "When this transaction is completed, I will make the first donation, a thousand dollars, to get things started."

Construction

After some months of haggling between lawyers, the property was donated to the Juvenile Ranch Rehabilitation Project, a nonprofit corporation set up to handle juvenile delinquents. Mason had been advised by lawyers from the state to go the nonprofit route. Mason then obtained private practice lawyers that were willing to donate their time to the project.

When the property was legally transferred, a board of directors was selected from volunteers interested in the project. Bill Mason, Bud Wilson, Judge Reynolds, Missus Abercrombie, and Missus Grundy were among those selected to serve on the board, although Missus Grundy strongly resisted. There were other members selected to the board, everyone willing to donate their time to the project.

Requests for donations were made to private businesses and individuals to raise money to start the project. Bill Mason was surprised. Some money was donated, but what surprised Bill was the number of individuals that were willing to donate their time and some materials to the project. Carpenters, plumbers, even some architects and people from other trades were willing to get involved.

A project manager was selected and the thousand dollars Missus Grundy donated and additional monies were used to buy materials to rebuild the house.

Inside the house, the kitchen was enlarged, the living room converted to a dining room, and an extra room was added to serve as an office. The two bedrooms were refurbished. The bathroom remained pretty much the same although new fixtures were installed.

Jimmy McIntyre had been out to the Grundy ranch before any

improvements were made and he was not impressed with the facility in its rundown condition. However, he visited on occasion as the work was being done and gradually started to favor the project improvements.

By the time the repairs to the house were completed, Jimmy had graduated from the university and moved onto the property. He'd been hired as the ranch manager as Mister Mason had wanted, although he had been warned by Mason on one of his frequent visits, "Until this project becomes fully developed, your paychecks might be few and far between. We're trying …"

"Am I going to starve out here?" interrupted Jimmy humorously.

"No," answered Mason, smiling. "As I was saying we're trying to hire a cook. We need to start work on a dormitory so we can start working with the young people. As soon as we have a facility to house these kids, we'll start to see a better cash flow. The state will pay us for each individual we take in, Judge Reynolds has seen to that and he's anxious to start sending us individuals that are involved in his courts."

"Has the judge pulled some political strings to ensure this project will succeed?"

"I'm sure he has," answered Mason, "but we don't need to discuss that. Since he was at the subcommittee hearing, he has shown a lot more interest in this project."

"Before we can take these kids in, even after the bunkhouse is built, we need to have some horses available that they can ride and take care of."

"That's true," replied Mason. "But there are still things that they can do, like repairing the corrals, fixing fence and the like."

"What about repairing the barn?"

"The barn is going to be torn down and completely rebuilt."

"I don't really have any carpenter skills to help with that, although I'm pretty good at tearing things apart," said Jimmy. "But I can start repairing fence and building corrals. However, I'd need a horse to ride while I'm fixing fence. I have a horse at the Wilson Ranch so I might take a couple of days and go over there and get him. And my saddle is over there."

"That will be fine," replied Mason. "There are some men coming to dig and set a foundation for the dormitory tomorrow. They know where to start digging, that's why those stakes are in the ground, and they will need to install a sewer system. Don't go to the Wilson's until they show up and get started."

"Right," answered Jimmy. "I'll look through the barn and see if there's some old fencing tools we can use to get started."

Jimmy found a wire stretcher, a roll of wire, and other miscellaneous tools in the barn. He had the thought that he needed to go through the barn before it was torn down and salvage whatever he thought would be needed in the future.

The next day while Jimmy was eating breakfast, a truck pulling a trailer with a backhoe on it pulled into the yard. Taking a cup of coffee with him, Jimmy went to meet the driver.

"Want a cup of coffee?" asked Jimmy.

"No," said the driver, as he got out of the truck. "We only have one day to do this and the boss said to get it done. This job is donated and he wants to get back to doing the profitable stuff. There are some other guys coming to set the cement forms."

Shortly, another truck pulled into the yard pulling a trailer loaded with the materials needed to make cement forms. Then a trailer pulling a camp trailer pulled into the yard.

Jimmy greeted the occupants of each vehicle and offered them coffee. Each declined except the driver of the truck with the camp trailer. "I can't do anything until those guys are well started," he said. "I'll have a cup with you. You must be Jimmy. I was told to ask for you."

"I'm Jimmy, you found the right person," he said, as they went to the house and Jimmy poured the driver a cup and refilled his own cup with coffee. They sat on the front porch drinking their coffee, watching the other men get started. Jimmy asked, "Why did you bring a camp trailer?"

"We'll set the forms today. There's a cement truck coming tomorrow to pour the foundation. I own this company, well, my brother and I own it, and I want to make sure everything is done right. I'll camp here until the cement cures."

"Are you bringing sick cement?" asked Jimmy.

"Sick cement? What do you mean?"

"You said the cement needed to cure," said Jimmy.

The owner of the cement company laughed. "I've had this company for a number of years and never heard that one. It's a good one! I'll have to tell my brother. You don't mind if I camp here, do you?"

"That sounds good to me," said Jimmy. "You'll be alone though. I've got to go get my horse and saddle and I'll be gone a couple of days. You could keep an eye on things."

"I'll do that. By the way, I'm Scott McPherson," he said, as he held out his hand.

Jimmy shook hands with Scott and said, "I'm Jimmy McIntyre."

Scott asked, grinning, "Irish?"

"Yep," answered Jimmy. Painfully aware of his black heritage, Jimmy quickly added, "I'm in disguise."

"You're all right, Jimmy. I'll bet you make a go of this venture."

"You know about this rehabilitation project?"

"Yes. Bill Mason filled me in when he convinced me to donate time, materials, and labor to this project. It sounds like a worthwhile endeavor to me."

"I hope it works," replied Jimmy.

"It will if you work hard at it. Bill Mason said this was a shaky venture financially. This might help you out," said Scott, as he reached for his wallet and pulled out a hundred-dollar bill.

"I don't know that I can take that," said Jimmy. "All the donations are supposed to go through the main office."

"Take it as a donation from me personally. The labor and materials are a company donation."

Jimmy took the hundred dollars and went to his new office. He made a note that Scott McPherson had donated the money on this date. He made a mental note to find out from Mason what he should do with any funds collected in the future. He got his bedroll and found Scott going to the work area. "I'm going to go get my horse. I'll be back in a couple of days," he yelled to Scott.

Scott just waved as Jimmy put his bedroll in the backseat, got in his car and started his trip to the Wilson Ranch. On the way, he did some thinking about his position at the ranch. He was manager, but he didn't really have anything to manage. He needed horses, saddles, and bridles along with pads and blankets. The more he thought about it, the more he determined what he needed if he was going to make this rehabilitation idea work. He began to have some self-doubts about his ability to manage a place. He'd never been a manager before, he only had the examples set by Bud Wilson and Honey. He wasn't sure he could adequately handle any situation that might come up.

He determined that the ranch would also need beds and bedding, a laundry facility, and he thought, *Lord only knows what else.*

When he got to town, he went directly to Bill Mason's office and found him busy counseling a youngster involved in probation. Mason's secretary announced his arrival and Mason promptly had him come in.

He introduced the youngster as Craig Richardson and Jimmy as the manager at the Juvenile Ranch Rehabilitation Project. Mason went on to say, "Craig might be a candidate for the ranch, once we have the dormitory completed."

"Well, that's good," said Jimmy. "They'd started digging the foundation as I left. It shouldn't be too long before the bunkhouse is done." Jimmy stressed the word bunkhouse. Jimmy didn't think it would be good to use the terms commonly used in rehabilitation programs. It would be better to use ranch terms where the ranch was involved. He made a mental note to discuss this in the future with Mason.

Craig Richardson didn't show much interest in Jimmy or the ranch information. He sat quietly with a sullen look on his face as if he didn't care whether he went to the ranch or not. His appearance reminded Jimmy of his days on probation before he went to the Wilson Ranch. He didn't have a good outlook on his future and this Richardson youngster appeared to be much the same.

Turning to Mason, Jimmy said, "Scott McPherson donated a hundred dollars to the project. I have it here."

Jimmy started to give the bill to Mason, but Mason, with a surprised look on his face said, "You better keep it. On your way back to the ranch, stop in at the local bank out there and start a checking account. You'll need to pay a few bills as we go. Any other donations you get, you can deposit them into that account. You've already gotten involved in fundraising, that's good."

"I didn't get involved in fundraising, he just gave it to me. I'm going to the Wilson's and get my horse and equipment, and then I'll be out at the ranch."

"I might come out and bring young Craig with me in the next couple of days," said Mason, "just to look things over."

"Bring a bedroll if you come. We've got the extra room and there's plenty of groceries. You might want to bring an air mattress, the only bed on the place is mine and I'm not giving it up!"

"Fine," said Mason, laughing. "How would you like to go to the ranch, Craig?"

Craig just shrugged his shoulders. Jimmy was familiar with Craig's indifference, he'd been there himself.

Jimmy then proceeded to the Wilson Ranch. He arrived just before supper and Bud invited him to eat with them. "Put your bedroll in the bunkhouse," said Bud.

Bud was used to Jimmy's unannounced visits and he was treated just like he was one of the family. It suddenly became aware to Jimmy that he considered Bud Wilson and the entire staff as family. In his familiarity with the Wilsons, he hadn't even shown the common courtesy to call ahead to see if it was all right that he come out. He needed to apologize to Bud for his lack of courtesy.

He met Honey and Pat at the barn.

"Jimmy McIntyre! What are you doing here?" Pat had seen him approach.

As Jimmy shook hands with Pat and Honey, he said, "I've come to get my saddle and make arrangements to get my horse. I've got a ranch to manage and don't have a horse to ride."

Honey asked, half joking, "How can you manage a ranch an' not have a horse to ride?"

"I'm aiming to fix that right directly," replied Jimmy.

"How is the ranch managing business going?" asked Pat.

"It's going really good," answered Jimmy. "I haven't had much to do—not all the construction is completed, there are no cattle or horses to look after, and none of the kids needing rehabilitation have showed up. I've been pretty busy doing nothing, so busy in fact that I haven't had time to enjoy it!" Pat and Honey laughed.

"I'll bet when that program gets well underway, you'll wish you didn't have anythin' to do," said Honey.

"You might be right," replied Jimmy.

"Your horse is out with our saddle horses. Do you want to help us bring them in?" asked Pat. "We've got an extra saddle horse we kept in."

"Certainly," said Jimmy, "you know I wouldn't miss it."

"Now that I've got two ranch managers lined out for the mornin's chores," said Pat, "I think I'll go to supper then retire."

"You better stick around," said Honey, "we might need your input regardin' ranch management after supper."

Jimmy and Pat laughed. Pat said, "You know, a hired man's work is never done havin' to keep management lined out." Everyone laughed.

At supper, Jimmy renewed his friendships with Sally, Ginny, Chet, Missus Abercrombie, and the cook. After supper Jimmy got Bud off to the side to make his apologizes. Bud listened as Jimmy made his amends then said, "There are no apologies necessary. I'm glad to hear you consider us family. You might not realize it, but we've considered you family for a long time. It's not necessary for you to call before you come out. You know there's always a place for you to stay and plenty to eat. You're always welcome."

The next day, Jimmy helped jingle the horses in. It occurred to him that this was the longest period of time in the spring and summer that he hadn't got horseback since he started to work on the Wilson Ranch a few years ago. He hadn't realized he missed it so much.

After the horses were corralled, Honey asked Jimmy, "How you gonna get your horse home? You ain't got a truck or trailer."

"I wanted to talk to you about that," answered Jimmy, as he unsaddled and turned loose the horse he had ridden. "You know your old truck, the dually one-ton with a stock rack? It's the one Rod taught me to drive when we went to get the mountain lion that Rod shot. Well, I was hoping you might sell it to me. We don't have a truck on the ranch and we really need one. Your old truck would fit the bill."

Honey replied, "I can't sell you the truck. It was given to me by my dad as a Christmas or graduation gift, I forget which, some years ago. There's a lot of sentimental value involved even though the truck ain't worth much. No, I can't part with it."

Jimmy was disappointed, but tried to hide his disappointment when he said, "I understand."

"Now," said Honey, "let's look over these saddle horses an' get yours caught up."

Jimmy wasn't long spotting his horse. He went to the barn and got his halter to catch the horse. When he returned, he stopped suddenly. *Why am I catching the horse?* he asked himself. *I don't have a way to get him to my ranch.*

"Get him caught up," said Honey.

"But I don't have a way to get him home," said Jimmy.

"I got a plan," said Honey.

A Real Ranch

Jimmy caught his horse and walked over to where Honey was standing.

"I been thinkin'," said Honey. "It's not good for a horse to be alone, they're herd animals. So, I'm goin' to give you another horse. Give me your horse an' get another halter from the barn. Then catch up Max. He's gettin' some age to him, but he's got a few years left."

"But …" protested Jimmy

"Just catch up Max," interrupted Honey.

"Do I detect a little confusion between two ranch managers? I'm here to straighten out things if necessary," said Pat, as he approached the two cowboys. He was grinning as he made his comment.

"No problems that us ranch managers can't solve. The junior ranch manager just doesn't want to do what he's told by the senior ranch manager."

Jimmy heard Honey's comment and immediately left to get a halter, then he caught Max and returned to where Honey and Pat were waiting for him, joking between themselves. The good-natured joking was always going on between those two. They worked well together. Jimmy got to thinking, *That's just one of the things I'll miss not being here in the future.*

"Now," said Honey, "my plan is to send Pat in the two-ton truck with those two horses over to your ranch."

Jimmy asked, "You are going to deliver the horses?"

"If I'm not mistaken, I think that's what I just said, but not me, I'm sendin' Pat," answered Honey.

"But it's a long day's drive over to my place," said Jimmy. "It will take you two days to go over and back."

"That's the beauty of my plan," replied Honey. "I'll send Pat and I'll be able to make some serious ranch management decisions unencumbered by unsolicited suggestions from the hired help. It will be just like havin' a workin' vacation for two days." Honey was smiling when he said that and Pat was laughing out loud.

Jimmy looked at these two cowboys in wonderment. There was always such good-natured joking going on between them. He concluded that was one of the reasons the ranch ran so smoothly.

Pat backed the two-ton truck up to the loading chute and they loaded the horses. Jimmy put his saddle and other gear into his car.

"Better put Max's saddle in the truck," said Honey. Jimmy got the saddle that was on the saddle rack that had Max's name on it. Max's bridle was looped over the horn and tied with the front saddle strings. He took the gear to the truck.

"Don't forget the pad and blanket," said Honey. Jimmy returned to the barn to get the pad and blanket and placed them on the side rack of the truck, then threw the saddle over them and tightened the cinch so the wind wouldn't blow them away. He noticed that there were a few bales of hay and a gunny sack, which he guessed was grain, in the corner of the bed of the truck.

Things were happening so fast that Jimmy was hard-pressed to keep up with them. He was given a horse and saddle to use on his ranch. The horse was a good dependable saddle horse that anyone could ride. He'd also been given some feed for the horses. He got to thinking that he couldn't take anything else from this ranch, he'd been given enough already. As he closed the tailgate on the truck, he said to Pat, "Better get your bedroll if you're going to spend the night at my place, and a cot. We don't have any beds or bedding yet."

"Listen to that," said Pat. "The junior ranch manager is already giving orders to the senior ranch hand! Do you think this ranch manager title is going to his head?"

Everyone laughed and Jimmy thought that he was being included in the good-natured joking. It occurred to him that this was family and he had always been included in it. He was going to miss them in the future. Pat did get a bedroll and put it in the front seat of the truck and a cot in the back.

He went to the lodge with Pat and Honey for breakfast. After they ate, Jimmy said his goodbyes to everyone and said, "It's time we got rolling. We've got a long drive ahead of us."

As they left the ranch with Pat following Jimmy in the two-ton truck, Jimmy regretted having to leave the Wilson Ranch. He didn't know when or if he would ever return.

By the time they got to the town outside of Jimmy's ranch, it was too late to go to the bank and start a checking account. They stopped at a café in town to have supper then went to the ranch. They unloaded the horses and tied them in the barn and threw them some hay.

"Better give them some grain so they know this is their new home," said Pat.

Without thinking, Jimmy said, "The senior ranch hand is giving orders to the new junior ranch manager already, huh?"

Pat looked surprised for a second then laughed. "I guess so," he said. The horses having been taken care of and Jimmy and Pat having eaten in town, the day's chores were completed. Pat carried his bedroll to the house and Jimmy brought the cot that had been put in the truck. Scott, who had camped at the ranch waiting for the cement to cure, greeted them as they left the barn.

Introductions were made and all three spent the early part of the evening visiting on the front porch of the house. Jimmy explained that this ranch consisted of about a hundred acres, sixty of which were planted in alfalfa and the rest was pasture.

Pat asked, "Are you an irrigator and a farmer?"

"No," replied Jimmy. "I've got to get acquainted with the neighbor who's been taking care of the hay and see what kind of arrangement we can make to continue the same agreement that Missus Grundy had to take care of the irrigating, mowing, and baling. We certainly can't afford to purchase the equipment we would need to farm this place.

"In the morning, if you're not in too big a rush to get back, we'll saddle the horses and I'll give you a guided tour around the ranch. It won't take long, it's a small ranch."

"I don't know how long Honey can get along without me, but I could take your tour," Pat said, laughing. "It's about time I got a guided tour rather than having to always be the guide."

They both laughed at Pat's comment. Scott, having been told of Pat's time spent on the Wilson Ranch, could appreciate Pat's comment and joined in on the laughter.

The next morning after breakfast they went to the barn and Jimmy was in a particularly good mood and ribbed Pat as they had been ribbing each other the night before. "Do you want me to saddle your horse for you?"

Pat, laughing, said, "It would be nice, but I'll bet I can still do that!"

"Well," said Jimmy, "when you get on, I'll adjust your stirrups for you."

"I'll bet I can have them about right before I get on." Pat saddled Max and took the stirrup and placed under his outstretched arm. His fingertips were about even with the swells of the saddle. "About two holes," he said.

Jimmy asked, "What do you mean?"

"I mean I've got to let this stirrup out two holes to have the stirrups at just about the right length." He let the stirrups out two holes on both sides and climbed into the saddle. He sat down, straightened the saddle, and then stood up in the stirrups. "Yep, that's about right."

Jimmy got on his horse and was surprised. The horse humped up and wanted to buck.

"Just let him stand there for a little bit," said Pat. "He ain't been ridden since last winter when you rode him at Christmas when you came out to visit. You should have untracked him first. I'll lead out and your horse should follow nice and easy."

"Yeah, I forgot," said Jimmy. "How come you guys haven't ridden him?"

"He's your horse," replied Pat. "You didn't say we could ride him, so we didn't."

It occurred to Jimmy that not only was he a member of the family at the Wilson Ranch, but he also was respected. He found a new admiration for his friends at the Wilson's.

Pat continued, "The new ranch manager needs to be thinking all the time to avert or prevent possible disasters. He can't afford to forget anything. This advice comes from the old ranch hand to the junior ranch manager."

Pat was smiling as he imparted this advice to Jimmy. Jimmy was listening carefully. Even though the advice was given in a humorous manner, the seriousness of it was not lost on him.

They started to leave the yard and Pat asked, "Which way do we go, boss? I don't want to get us lost on your first ride out here!" Pat was maintaining the humor of the situation.

Jimmy's horse was walking gingerly, not having been ridden for some months. "Go east," said Jimmy. "As soon as my horse works out the kinks, I'll lead us around the place. He should be all right by the time we hit the alfalfa."

"That looks like a good stand of hay," said Pat, when they reached the hay. "It looks like it's about ready to be cut."

"I'll ride over to the neighbor's tomorrow and see what it will take to get it cut. I can lead now, my horse has settled down. Even though we're still within sight of the ranch house, I don't want you to get us lost. We still need to ride through the pasture."

"Good," said Pat. "Old Max here isn't used to leading. Did you see him shy at everything? Why, I almost fell off!"

Max hadn't shied at anything and Jimmy doubted that any horse on the Wilson Ranch could have thrown Pat. Pat was joking, much in the same manner he had witnessed between him and Honey. Jimmy had the thought that Pat had actually accepted him as manager of the ranch and he felt good about that and it did much to relieve the self-doubt he had been experiencing.

They rode around the hayfield and into the pasture, talking about the possibilities of the ranch and how to handle some of the problems that might arise. Jimmy listened intently as they talked, not wanting to miss an opportunity to learn something.

A good part of the conversation was about buying horses at a horse sale. "How many horses do you think you'll need?" asked Pat.

"The ranch will initially be set up to handle ten juveniles with a cook, me, and another individual to supervise. I think we will need a dozen or so, maybe more. We'll need an extra horse or two in case one comes up lame. We'll have to see how it goes."

"When you get to buyin' horses through the sale," said Pat, "be careful! You can't always tell when a horse has been drugged. Show up early and look everything over good. If you get a chance, you ride everything you plan on buying, and watch when the horses are ridden through the ring. If you get the chance, talk to the owner who's selling the horse. There's always a reason a horse is being sold. Some of the reasons are valid, some are not. Often it's better to buy a horse from an individual rather than through a sale, but be careful of the professional horse traders. If you find one you can trust, do business with him and stay away from the others. There are a lot of unscrupulous horse traders out there. And remember, color doesn't make a good horse!"

Yes, he had learned plenty in college, but he was having the chance to learn something from someone who had actually done ranch work. There was a big difference between learning something out of a book and learning it from the back of a horse.

They reached the far end of the pasture and Jimmy spied a wire gate in the fence. "I guess," said Jimmy, "this is where they hit the trail that takes them to the National Forest. If that's so, I'll need to put in a swinging gate here so we can ride through it without having to get off a horse to open and close it. I'll have to go up there and learn the trails before we take any dudes up there."

"You mean juvenile delinquents, don't you?"

"Yeah, I forgot again," said Jimmy, somewhat embarrassed.

"Don't let it bother you," said Pat. "It proves you're human."

"But you and Honey never forget anything," rebutted Jimmy.

"Ah … yes we do. But we work together and more or less cover each other. We both know what needs to be done. And don't forget Sally, she had to correct Honey with the dudes more than once. She did it with finesse and nobody noticed. When someone did notice, they made fun of it and it passed. And remember, Honey had more experience than you, hence he forgot less."

"I've still got a lot to learn even though I've got a college education," said Jimmy.

"You maintain that attitude all your life and you'll learn more than you expect," replied Pat. "We'd better be headed back. I've still got a long drive back to the Wilson Ranch. As it is, I won't get back until after dark."

Jimmy looked at his watch. "You're right. And I still have to go to town and open a checking account for the ranch in addition to visiting with the neighbors. I guess I'll drive over there, rather than ride my horse, although I'd rather ride my horse."

"You might make a manager," said Pat. "You're figuring out the best, most efficient way to do something."

"But the Wilson's did all they could horseback," said Jimmy.

"That's right. But the jobs that needed to be done horseback were done horseback and many were done horseback simply to keep the dudes busy."

They rode back to the ranch talking. When they got to the ranch, they unsaddled the horses and tied them in the barn. Pat put his bedroll and the cot in the truck, shook hands with Jimmy and said, "Keep in touch."

"I'll buy your dinner in town," said Jimmy, not wanting his friend to leave. "I've got to go to the bank anyway."

Pat, sensing Jimmy's reluctance to see him leave declined the invitation, saying, "Nope, I'm late already. I'll drive right through." He got in the truck and without a backward glance, drove off.

Jimmy felt strangely alone until Scott came over and said, "A good friend of yours, huh?"

"Yes," said Jimmy, "better than I had thought. I've got to go to town, you need anything?"

"If you get a couple of steaks, I'll barbeque 'em for supper at my trailer."

"You're on," said Jimmy. He went to the car and followed Pat into town. On the way he thought, *We've got a real ranch now. We've got two horses. We're not a one-horse outfit!* He laughed at the thought.

The Neighbors

Jimmy went directly to the bank when he got to town and opened the checking account with the hundred-dollar bill Scott had given him. He opened the account under the name Juvenile Ranch Rehabilitation Project—a long and, he thought, impressive title. He was told the imprinted checks would be mailed to him at the ranch.

He went to the grocery store and bought some sirloin steaks and other grocery items. Then he headed to the neighbor's place to see about getting hay cut. He found the neighbor's place from the main road and the name on the mailbox was Burkhart.

He found Missus Burkhart at the house, but her husband wasn't present. "Richard is irrigating out in the fields," said Missus Burkhart.

"Do you mind if I walk out and talk with him?"

"Certainly not, he's over there somewhere," replied the woman, pointing to the south. She shut the door curtly and Jimmy started walking in the direction she had pointed.

As he walked, he wondered at the curt reception by Missus Burkhart, and questioned whether his skin color had anything to do with it. He hoped Mister Burkhart, Richard she'd called him, would be more sociable. And, he thought, *Richard seemed a little formal. Why didn't she just refer to him as Dick, or something less formal, like "my husband"?*

Jimmy found Richard Burkhart about half a mile from the house, pulling a canvas dam from an irrigation ditch. He'd put another dam in farther down the ditch and made his cutouts. As the water rushed to the next dam, he started to fill in the old cutouts.

He was busy working and didn't notice Jimmy approaching. He looked startled when Jimmy said, "Mister Burkhart?"

Jimmy extended his hand but Burkhart ignored it as he took a look at Jimmy and went back to filling in the cutouts that had been used.

Undaunted, Jimmy said, "I'm Jimmy McIntyre. It looks like we're going to be neighbors."

"You buy the Grundy place?"

"No," replied Jimmy. "I'm the manager of the Juvenile Ranch Rehabilitation Project."

"Juvenile delinquents running wild all over the country, unsupervised? Can't be any good come from it," retorted Burkhart.

"The youngsters won't be running wild," said Jimmy. "They'll be supervised."

"Can't be any good come from it," repeated Burkhart. "Young criminals, that's all they are. Once they've done wrong and find out how easy it is to get away with it, they'll keep doing it."

Jimmy felt his temper rising, but he controlled himself. He was tempted to tell his own story, but decided against it. Instead, he said, "These kids are not hardened criminals. They just need a fair shot in life and some positive direction. If they don't get that, they could easily become hardened criminals."

"What do you want from me?" Burkhart didn't stop to listen, but continued to fill in a cutout and move to the next one. Jimmy was following him on the other side of the ditch. Their conversation was moving, but along the ditch, as Jimmy said, "We have about sixty acres of hay that needs to be cut. I'd like to work out an agreement whereby you cut and bale the hay for a percentage. We're open at this point to …"

"Your agreement has already been tended to," interrupted Burkhart. "Who do you think has been irrigating the hay and cutting it over the past few years? I have!"

"I knew that a neighbor had been taking care of the place, but didn't know which one," said Jimmy, thinking that Burkhart didn't take very good care of the place, letting the corrals and barn become run down like they had. He decided not to mention the condition of the corrals and barn. Jimmy continued, "We'd like to thank you for the excellent care of the hayfield you have provided."

"Well," said Burkhart, "I had to take good care of it. Part of it is mine. Missus Grundy informed me of her plans to donate her place to you people and I tried to talk her out of it, but couldn't. If I'd have had the money, I'd have bought it long ago. Our agreement was that I maintain the hayfield and in return I get a percentage of the hay crop. The percentage that went to her was used to feed the ten cows and calves of hers that I run with my cows. It was a sixty-forty deal with her getting the sixty percent. She's a shrewd old bird, sharp as a tack. She has indicated that the deal remain the same with you people until I've paid off some money she lent me a while back."

Jimmy asked, "Does this mean you're going to cut the hay and bale it?"

"What do you think I just said, boy?"

Jimmy bristled at being called "boy" but didn't say anything. He didn't know if the term referred to his skin color or his age. He was quite a bit younger than Burkhart, who he figured to be in his seventies.

"She also said that the cattle were to be turned over to you when they came off the forest in the fall."

"I was unaware of that," said Jimmy.

"There's a lot of things you're not aware of, youngster," said Burkhart.

When Burkhart used the term "youngster," Jimmy thought his earlier use of the word "boy" referred to his age. He found it strange that he was becoming more aware of racial references than he had been in the past.

"When do you figure on cutting the hay?"

"As soon as I've finished cutting mine," answered Burkhart.

"If I can help, just let me know, Mister Burkhart. I'll be on the place making repairs most of the time. It's good to meet you," said Jimmy as he turned to leave.

"Yeah," said Burkhart, as he returned to his irrigating.

Jimmy had found Burkhart antagonistic and pondered it driving back to the ranch. He didn't know if it was because of his skin color or because of an inherent distrust of juvenile delinquents harbored by Burkhart. He had tried to leave Burkhart's place on a friendly note, volunteering to help if needed, but didn't know how his offer had been taken. He decided not to worry about the situation, he had enough to do without something else to worry about.

When he got back to the ranch he found Scott anxiously waiting the arrival of the steaks. He'd plumb forgot about the barbeque.

"I thought you'd got lost," said Scott.

"No, I just had more to do than I figured." Jimmy made a mental note to himself, *time management.* Pat had said that was part of being a manager.

Scott took the steaks and Jimmy put the other groceries in the house. While they ate Jimmy continued to ponder the neighbor situation. Even though he'd concluded not to worry about it, the situation bothered him.

The next morning after breakfast, Scott started taking down the cement forms. The cement had cured and as soon as the forms were removed and the space around the foundation was back-filled, construction on the bunkhouse could begin.

Jimmy found some poles behind the barn and mended the corral so he could turn the horses loose. The horses seemed to appreciate this. When he turned them loose, they went to the middle of the corral and promptly rolled. *That will make life easier for them,* thought Jimmy. They could get water themselves rather than having to be led to water twice a day.

About ten in the morning two trucks pulled into the yard. Jimmy recognized the first truck—it had the backhoe on a trailer. The second truck pulled an empty flatbed trailer. As soon the cement forms were disassembled and loaded on to the empty trailer, the man on the backhoe started filling in the hole.

When the backhoe was done back-filling, it was loaded on the trailer and they pulled out. Scott hooked up his trailer as the other trucks left. He'd be the last one to leave after he said goodbye.

Scott came to Jimmy. "It's time to go," he said. "I do want to thank you for letting me camp here. This little vacation is just what I needed."

Jimmy said, "Thanks for the barbeque!" He was tempted to say to come anytime, but he didn't invite him back. He thought when the kids started arriving, it might be wise to restrict visitors to the ranch. Again, he made a mental note to discuss this with Mason the next time he saw him. He was making so many mental notes that he decided to get a pencil and paper to carry in his pocket.

Scott left and all of the sudden he felt alone. "Well," he said, talking to himself, "I'm the manager of a ranch, but I don't have anything to manage but myself. I guess I ought to get started doing something, fix fence I suppose. But first, I need to go to the house and get some paper and a pencil."

He caught his horse, saddled him, and contemplated catching Max and using him as a packhorse. He decided to go without Max and just took a hammer and a bag of staples. He planned on just knocking in the top wire and seeing how much repair work was actually needed before taking a lot of equipment. *If I'm lucky, I won't need to bring a lot. I'd like to be able to turn the horses out on pasture, I'm running short of hay.*

Jimmy rode the pasture fence. He decided he'd have to put a fence in between the hayfield and the pasture. In building this fence, he decided to construct a lane along the top of the hayfield to the corrals so the horses couldn't get into the hay when they were turned out at night and brought in the next day. He thought he could use steel posts to make the lane and promptly made a note. He roughly estimated that one every twelve feet should be good and thought he'd need about ten posts to make the lane. A swinging gate at the pasture end of the lane would work to keep the horses on the pasture overnight. He wrote down "1–12-foot gate." Then he wrote down "4 rolls barbed wire."

His list was getting longer as he thought about what he needed— wire, steel posts, clips to fasten the wire to the steel posts, stays to place between the steel posts, and a post pounder. He thought a more thorough search of the barn might provide some of the items needed and resolved to search the barn the next day. On a whim, he added to his list, "truck."

For the most part, the outside fence needed little repair. Where the wires sagged a little, he could tighten them up by kinking the wire on itself. This would work for a year or so, but would need to be permanently fixed at a later date. His fence fixing was accomplished in a couple of hours and he noted on his paper that the outside fence could use more repairs in the fall.

He returned to the ranch to find Mason and the youngster, Craig Richardson, at the corrals looking at Max. Jimmy rode his horse up to them and greeted them with a "Howdy!" He thought he was applying the western touch a little heavy and grinned at himself.

Mason responded with a "Howdy! You remember Craig here, don't you?"

"Sure do," replied Jimmy. He stuck his hand through the corral poles and said, "How you doing?"

Craig extended a limp hand and shook Jimmy's. "Okay, I guess," he replied. "These your horses?"

"Yep."

"What are their names?"

"This one, I just call him Digger. The other one is Max. They're both pretty good horses. Do you ride?"

"No," answered Craig.

Jimmy continued to question Craig, trying to get better acquainted.

Craig was uncommunicative. His answers were short—he wasn't volunteering any information.

Jimmy recalled his days in juvenile detention and could relate to Craig's feelings. Mason remained quiet, letting Jimmy direct the conversation, what there was of it.

Finally, Mason said, "We've looked around in the house and you're a pretty fair housekeeper, Jimmy. Everything is in place and surprisingly, there aren't any dirty dishes in the sink."

"The best time to do a job is when it needs to be done," said Jimmy. "If you let your chores pile up, pretty soon you have more chores to do than your regular job." Mason laughed. Craig just looked at Jimmy.

"The foundation for the bunkhouse has been poured and construction can begin at any time you're ready," said Jimmy. "Those holes and trenches in the ground that haven't been back-filled are for the sewer system. When that gets done, I guess we'll have to fill it in by hand."

Craig asked, "Can I pet your horse?"

"Sure," said Jimmy. "Climb over the fence and come in here and get acquainted."

"I don't want to come in there," said Craig. It was apparent that Craig was afraid of horses.

"It's okay," said Jimmy. "He's a nice horse and he likes to be petted."

Apprehensively, Craig climbed the fence and jumped down on the inside. The movement spooked Jimmy's horse and he shied backward. Craig started to scramble up the fence.

Jimmy stopped him by grabbing the back of his belt. "It's all right. The horse is more afraid of you than you are of him." He held on to his horse with the reins.

Slowly, Craig maneuvered his way slowly down the fence. "That's good," said Jimmy. "You always want to move kinda slowly around horses. They don't know what to expect from everybody. Here, you take the reins and just walk up to him."

Craig clearly was afraid of the horse, and reluctantly took the reins from Jimmy. "He knows you're afraid of him," said Jimmy, and trying to remember what Honey had told him years ago, added, "Fear of a horse is not necessary, but a healthy respect is."

Craig slowly walked to the horse with his hand outstretched. The horse just stood there, having recovered from his shying when Craig jumped down, and he watched Craig approach him. Craig's outstretched hand finally touched the horse's nose and the horse wrinkled his nose. Craig instinctively pulled his hand back.

"Just pet him, don't tickle him," said Jimmy, laughing. Mason was laughing also. Craig extended his hand and petted the horse.

While Mason was laughing, Jimmy thought it would be a good

time to present his list of needs to him. Mason took the paper and looked it over. When he got to the end, he exclaimed, "A truck! We can't afford a new truck! These other items, we might get a hardware store to donate them, but we can't buy a new truck."

"Well," said Jimmy, "we need one. I can't be driving my car through the sagebrush loaded with fencing supplies and such. And we ought to get a flatbed truck with removable sides so we can use it to haul horses and hay. We also need more horses to keep the kids busy when they come."

"You've got two horses now," said Mason. "Where'd the other one come from?"

"He was given to me by Honey at the Wilson's. He's a solid old dude horse. Honey also gave me a saddle for the horse. We'll also need saddles and bridles, blankets and pads for the horses. We're just getting started, but we will need all this in the future."

"We've already started," said Mason. "Craig here is our first client, ah … participant in our program. He can stay out here if you've got room for him."

"Our bunkhouse isn't done yet, heck it isn't even started," said Jimmy. "The foundation was just poured a few days ago. But he can stay in the other bedroom in the house if he wants to stay."

"He doesn't have a choice. That decision is up to you," said Mason, reaching for some papers inside his coat. He handed the papers to Jimmy.

The thought occurred to Jimmy that Mason looked out of place on the ranch dressed in a suit and tie. Then he realized that Mason was on official business.

The papers Mason had in his pocket were official papers assigning Craig to the Juvenile Ranch Rehabilitation Project. They were signed by Judge Reynolds. As Jimmy looked over the papers, he noticed that he was to become responsible for Craig. He realized that Mason's visit was to place Craig out on the ranch and not just a friendly visit.

He turned to Craig and asked, "Do you want to stay out here?"

Craig was hesitant in his answer. "I … I don't know. I guess so."

"Good! We need some help here. There's more to do than I

can handle alone." Jimmy tried to sound as if the youngster was to become a working part of the ranch rather than a guest. "Can you cook?"

"No," answered Craig.

"Well, I can't either," replied Jimmy.

"But I don't want to starve," replied Craig.

"We won't starve," answered Jimmy, "but we might not eat so well."

Mason said, "I've been looking for a cook but so far haven't found anyone acceptable."

"Acceptable! All we need is someone who can cook," replied Jimmy. "I'm getting tired of doing my own cooking and I hate it. Actually, I should rephrase that; I don't mind doing my own cooking, the part I hate is having to eat it!"

Mason laughed and Jimmy noticed Craig trying to control a laugh.

"We need someone that has a clean background, no criminal record, no signs of alcoholism or drug use to fill this position out here," said Mason. "We need to give this program more than an even chance to succeed. The individual we hire to cook must be able to add to our program in a positive manner. I'll keep looking until we find a suitable applicant then send him out to you for your approval."

"My approval?"

"Yes," answered Mason. "We need a consensus and agreement among all parties concerned. We need someone who has or can develop a genuine interest in the welfare of these boys and the outcome of their stay here."

Jailbird

Jimmy took the papers from Mason and questioned the meaning of them, particularly the part that said he was responsible for Craig.

"Does this mean I'm his probation officer?" he asked.

"Not exactly," replied Mason. "I'm still his probation officer. These papers make you a person in a supervisory capacity."

"You've come prepared to leave him?"

"Yes," answered Mason. "His sleeping bag and what clothes he has are in the extra bedroom in the house. He's set to stay here. The judge has indicated that if he stays, with your approval, he can proceed with the paperwork necessary to pay the program for his expenses. We're almost in business!"

Jimmy signed the papers. He asked, "Bill, can you cook?"

Mason looked at him. "Are you inviting me to dinner if I can cook?"

"It's supper," replied Jimmy, "and the answer is yes."

"Well," replied Mason, "I'm not really prepared to stay. I need to get back to the office tonight, even though I'll be late getting there. Oh, by the way, write down the horse and equipment donated by Honey. We'll need to send them some sort of receipt they can use for tax purposes. You'll need to keep track of everything donated out here and submit it to me once a month. We'll need to keep detailed records. I need to be going."

"Wait until I unsaddle my horse and I'll see you to your car," said Jimmy.

"Good," said Mason, "I've got some more papers for you."

Jimmy unsaddled his horse. As he walked around the rear of

the horse, Craig, who had been watching, said, "Aren't you afraid the horse will kick you?"

"No," replied Jimmy. "The horse knows what I'm doing. And I have my hand on his rump to let him know where I am."

Jimmy thought this might be a good time to start Craig's education. "There's two kinds of people in this world. There's the kind that says, 'This horse can't kick me' and he's standing right behind the horse close to him, with his hand on his rump. Then," he said, moving away from the horse a good twenty feet or so, "there's the kind that says 'That horse can't kick me either.' They're both right. The difference is that the guy right next to the horse knows horses and the guy that's away from the horse don't."

Jimmy hung the cinch from the cinch keeper on the off side of the saddle, walked around the horse, unbridled him, pulled the saddle and blankets and put them in the barn. Craig followed. Jimmy pointed to the other saddle in the barn and said, "You can ride that saddle tomorrow." Even though he'd just rode the fence, he said, "We'll ride fence tomorrow."

Craig didn't say anything.

At Mason's car, Mason gave Jimmy a file. "This is Craig's file. You need to document it as you go along and return it to me when he leaves. Of course, as Craig is a juvenile, this is all confidential information, not to be made public. I'll send out a filing cabinet and you can keep it and other papers locked in it."

"It looks like there's going to be a lot of paperwork involved with this job," said Jimmy.

"There is," replied Mason, "but it's all necessary."

"One other thing before you leave," said Jimmy. "I met the neighbors, the Burkhart's. They don't seem too cooperative. Mister Burkhart is supposed to take care of the hay and he's done a good job so far, but he's not too pleased about having juvenile delinquents around."

"Missus Grundy told me about him," said Mason. "She said he was difficult to get along with but was basically honest and would hold to his word. I'll talk to her some more about him." Mason left to go back to his office.

"The day's about shot," said Jimmy. "Let's go see what we can rustle up for supper."

"Rustle up? Are we going to steal something to eat?"

"No," laughed Jimmy. "It's just a term used on ranches."

Supper that night consisted of a couple of cans of beef stew heated on the stove. Craig was quiet as they ate their supper.

After supper Jimmy said, "I'll wash and you dry."

"Then what?" queried Craig.

"Then we'll sit out on the porch and relax and watch the sun go down. Maybe we'll get better acquainted."

"No television?"

"Nope."

"It must be boring around here without a TV."

"It really isn't," said Jimmy. "At the end of the day we'll be so tired, we'll look forward to getting some sleep."

As they sat out on the porch, Jimmy looked over the file on Craig that Mason had left him. It was an extensive file, documenting Craig's court appearances with Judge Reynolds' notations and Bill Mason's actions. The last entry read, "Sentenced to the Juvenile Ranch Rehabilitation Project." Mason had noted, "If this doesn't work, it's probably reform school for the youngster."

Jimmy read the last notation very seriously. He said to Craig, "You've got an extensive record here."

"I got a rotten deal," said Craig. "That stuff is all lies."

Jimmy let Craig's comment pass. He thought it best to establish a good relationship with the youngster. "Your record is almost as extensive as mine was."

Craig looked at Jimmy with renewed interest. "You mean you're a juvenile delinquent, too?"

Jimmy laughed. "I'm not a juvenile delinquent, not any more. But I used to be. I'm convinced that if I'd have stayed on the path I was traveling, I'd be a criminal today, probably behind bars, incarcerated for only God knows how long."

"What did you get caught doing?"

"Pretty much the same stuff you've been doing. Petty theft— stealing cigarettes, beer, and the like. Stealing anything I wanted, actually. I did a lot of fighting in school and I sluffed school a lot. My record is longer than yours. Looks like we're both a couple of jailbirds. How old are you?"

"Thirteen," answered Craig. "You ever do any drugs? That's where the real money is."

Jimmy noticed that he had seemed to capture Craig's attention. "No," answered Jimmy. "I was always afraid of them. I see here you've gotten caught with drugs in your possession. What kind of drugs?"

"Just pot," answered Craig.

"Tomorrow while we're riding fence, I want you to look at the fence and think of it as a chain link fence, ten or twelve feet high with barbed wire on top of it, like a prison fence."

"You mean this is a prison?"

"No," laughed Jimmy. "The fence we're riding is designed to keep cattle or horses in or out, not people. The prison fences are meant to control people. You be thinking about having to spend the rest of your life behind a chain link fence. Every time I go out to fix fence, the thought of living behind a chain link fence crosses my mind. I'm grateful I'm not living that way today."

After some more discussion about Craig's past, Jimmy said, "It's time to hit the sack. We've got to get up early in the morning."

The next morning after breakfast, Jimmy saddled the horses. As he saddled Digger, he was careful to teach Craig how to do it. "Pay close attention Craig, you'll be doing this for yourself tomorrow, or next time we ride. And I expect we'll be riding every day."

Even though Jimmy had ridden the fence the day before, he decided to do it again just to keep Craig busy. Craig was not a horseman, having never ridden before. He struggled into the saddle. Jimmy thought it wise to spend some time giving Craig some instruction, so he conducted a riding lesson in the corral. He started by telling Craig what to do, then he showed him and then he had Craig do it. The lesson went well and Craig seemed to pick up on it quickly.

He grabbed the bag of staples and a hammer and they started out. He also got the fence stretcher. When Jimmy had ridden the fence the day before, he'd only stapled up the top wire; the one he could reach from horseback. With Craig along, they would get off the horses and fix the fence properly. They could tie the horses to the fence posts or hobble them while they worked. Thinking this would be a more extensive job than what he had done yesterday, he got a couple of canteens and filled them with water. They were set and headed out.

When they got to the outside fence, Jimmy decided to hobble the horses and let them graze while they fixed fence. He could save some feed back at the ranch.

Craig watched the horses as Jimmy turned them loose. Their movements were restricted by the hobbles. They had to raise up a little, then move both feet forward at the same time. To Craig, they appeared to be struggling. He asked, "Are they fighting them things?"

"The hobbles?" answered Jimmy.

"Yes."

"No," replied Jimmy, "they've been broke to hobbles. They're used to them."

"Broke?"

"Trained might be better word," said Jimmy. "The hobbles just restrict their movements a little and slow them down. Once they learn about them, they can get around pretty good. It's kinda like being on probation. They've got some freedom, but if they make a mistake, they get caught."

They set about fixing fence. Jimmy did most of the work, but Craig was willing when told what to do. Craig did spend a lot of time watching the horses and their strange movements as they grazed.

About noon, they took a break. Jimmy sent Craig to catch the horses and bring back the canteens. Craig approached each horse very slowly and cautiously. He was still nervous around them. The horses, being used to hobbles and humans, just stood still and let Craig get the canteens.

"We should have brought some lunch," said Jimmy. "You hungry?"

"Yeah," answered Craig.

"Well, we'll be done here before too long. Then we'll knock off and get an early supper."

"This fence fixing ain't too bad a job," said Craig. "But anyone could climb over that fence and leave anytime."

"The fence isn't meant to hold people," said Jimmy. "It's meant to hold cattle and horses. Have you been comparing it to a chain link fence?"

"I guess so," answered Craig.

"Well," said Jimmy, "you could climb this fence and leave anytime you want. But where would you go? It's fifteen or twenty miles into town and you'd get picked up before too long. Then you'd find out what it's like to live behind a chain link fence, ten or twelve feet high, with barbed wire on the top."

Jimmy could see that Craig was listening and paying attention, so he added, just in case Craig was contemplating an unauthorized leave, "You can leave here anytime you want. But if you leave without my permission or Mister Mason's, you'll be caught eventually and spend some time behind bars. If you decide you want to leave, legally, we'll call Mason, he'll come and get you and then it's up to him what you'll do. Him and Judge Reynolds. You think about it because you'll learn here that you're responsible for your own actions."

Craig seemed to be contemplating what Jimmy had said as they fixed fence.

They finished the fence and rode back to the ranch. Jimmy was satisfied with the condition of the fence and scratched off on his notepaper the part about repairing the fence in the fall. He changed that to repairing the fence in the spring.

Jimmy told Craig to watch carefully as he unsaddled his horse. "Do this with your horse exactly as I'm doing it to mine," he said. Then he watched as Craig unsaddled Max. "Make sure you always undo the breast collar first, then the back cinch, then the main cinch. There have been a lot of wrecks because someone didn't undo everything in the right order and there's never any good that comes from it. Generally, when that happens, equipment gets torn up pretty bad."

Supper that night consisted of hamburgers, something Jimmy could fix easily. While they were eating, Craig asked, "What do we have to do tomorrow?"

"I think we need to go through the barn and clean it out. Anything we can use we'll keep. Anything we can't use, we'll throw away. The barn is going to be torn down and replaced. When the new barn is built, we'll build some new corrals. We might have to take a ride up on the forest. I've never been there and I need to do some exploring."

After supper was done, Jimmy said, "Let's see now, I washed last night and you dried, so tonight, you wash and I'll dry. Make sure you get them dishes clean!"

The next day they started on the barn. They found some rolls of barbed wire, a few more steel posts, a steel post driver and some more miscellaneous tools. They piled everything they could use in one of the stalls and what they didn't want, they piled outside.

"When we get a truck, we'll take this to the dump," said Jimmy.

In the afternoon, they saddled the horses and went to the gate at the end of the pasture that bordered the National Forest. The trail on the forest was well marked although it hadn't been used for some time. They rode through groves of aspen trees and it was cooler than riding out in the open. The grass was good in the aspen and they saw signs of some cattle, but didn't see any cows. Higher up in the meadows, bordered by lodgepole pines, they saw quite a few cows with calves by their sides. After a few hours of riding on the forest, they headed back toward the ranch. This was a big country and Jimmy decided it would need more exploring in the future. There would be plenty of riding for him and young Craig.

When they got back to the ranch, Craig stiffly got off his horse. He limped when he walked. Jimmy had to laugh. He remembered his first rides at the Wilson Ranch and how he must have looked when he got off his horse.

"Not used to riding, huh?"

"That's right," said Craig. "I've got muscles I didn't know I had!"

"You'll get used to riding," said Jimmy. "The more you do it, the easier it becomes. But we did spend a long time out there, five hours is a lot of riding if you're not used to it. I apologize. I should have been more considerate."

"Considerate of me? And you're apologizing to me?"

"Yes," replied Jimmy, "I should have thought about it."

"Nobody ever apologized to me before and nobody was ever considerate of me before."

"Well, Craig, hopefully you'll learn a new way of life out here. When you're considerate of others, they'll be considerate of you. To show you how consideration works, we'll give it a try right here. I've cooked supper the last two nights, now it's your turn!" Jimmy was laughing when he made his last comment.

Craig had a big smile when he said, "You might not be so considerate of me after you eat what I cook. I've never cooked."

"There's no time like the present to learn. I'll be here to direct you, but you'll do it."

Supper was a long time coming, even though Jimmy directed Craig in his efforts "Don't be afraid to read the directions on the cans or packages," advised Jimmy. "And it's best to follow instructions."

Supper consisted of fried potatoes, fried meat, and fried hominy. The meat was burnt, the potatoes only half-cooked, and the hominy hot. But it was edible, to some degree. While they were eating, Jimmy asked, "What do you call this mess?"

"I don't have a name for it," said Craig. "I've never done this before."

"From now on it'll be known as 'Craig's Mess.' I'll fix it tomorrow and show you how to fix it properly. Now, who washes and who dries?"

After the dishes were washed and dried, they sat out on the front porch to watch the sun go down and visit a little. As they were watching the sun set, the phone rang. Jimmy answered with, "Juvenile Ranch Rehabilitation Project. Can I help you?" He was surprised to hear Bill Mason's voice on the other end.

"Jimmy! Where have you been? I've been trying to get a hold of you all day!" Mason sounded frustrated.

"We do have some chores and odd jobs to do around here

and we've been doing them," answered Jimmy, somewhat sarcastically. He wondered what was up. It was after hours for Mason, he was calling from his home phone. "How can I help you this fine evening?"

"We'll need to get you an answering machine for the phone so we can stay in contact," said Mason. "We've got …"

"A cook to stay at the ranch, cook and answer the phone would be better," interrupted Jimmy. "Craig's cooking has about done me in." Jimmy was smiling when he said that and Craig, standing in the doorway, smiled.

"Can Craig cook? Have you got him cooking for you?"

"No! He can't cook. We're taking turns cooking. I really can't wait for my turn tomorrow."

"That's good. Yes, I'm still looking for a cook," replied Mason. "But what I called about is that we've got a truck with a septic tank coming tomorrow. There'll be pipe for the drain field coming also. The driver will unload the tank and hook up the drain field. You'll have to fill in the trenches after the pipe is installed. He'll be there early, so don't leave the ranch."

"We expect to be here all day," replied Jimmy.

"Where were you this morning?"

"We rode out on the National Forest to see if we could find any of Missus Grundy's cows."

"Did you see any?"

"No," answered Jimmy. "The cattle we did see all looked to be in good shape and Grundy's cows should be in good shape also."

"We can worry about them later," replied Mason. "When the sewer system is installed, we can start construction on the dormitory. I've got …"

"Bunkhouse," interrupted Jimmy. Jimmy could see that Mason was having a hard time distinguishing between the ranch and a detention center.

"Ah, yes, bunkhouse. Well, we've convinced a lumber company to donate the materials needed to put up a frame and the rafters. We still need to get the siding and some carpenters to put it all together. This deal is coming together, but slowly."

"Apparently we're making some progress," said Jimmy.

"Yes. I forwarded the paperwork to Judge Reynolds and he has approved it. He informed me that we should be getting monthly a check for Craig's stay beginning on the first of the month. It'll be coming to your address, so deposit it in the ranch's account."

Jimmy smiled. Mason had been a probation officer for so long he was used to giving detailed instructions to everyone.

"As soon as the dormitory, ah, that is bunkhouse is completed, we can enroll a few more youngsters in our program and begin to see a little more money come in from the state. Even though this is a nonprofit venture, we need money to operate."

"Yes," said Jimmy, "and money to buy a flatbed pickup. We cleaned out the barn and there's a big pile of junk out in the yard that needs to go to the dump. Right now it's pretty unsightly."

"I'm working on that, too," said Mason. "There's a lot that I'm working on, but I don't have the time. This project is like having a second job, and I'm overworked in my first job."

"Don't get discouraged, Bill. All this will come together when it's supposed to." Jimmy thought it strange that he was giving his former probation officer encouragement and smiled at the idea.

"I'm not discouraged," replied Mason. "We've just got a lot to do and sometimes I wonder if we'll get it all done. Stay close to the ranch tomorrow. Goodbye."

Mason hung up and Jimmy pondered the plight he was in. Trying to establish a ranch without any money was difficult, but it had been done in the past. Of course those days were during the nineteenth century, or was it the twentieth century? It was after the Civil War and Texas longhorn cattle ranged free all over the West. It had been done before, but times were different today. And this was a different kind of ranch, one whose main purpose was not cattle, but rehabilitation of wayward youngsters.

Filling In

Jimmy was up early the next day and had to wake Craig for breakfast. A few days of some physical labor plus better than half a day riding was starting to show on the youngster. He hadn't done any physical labor before and this was good for him.

"We don't have much to do today," said Jimmy. "Mister Mason said that a septic tank was being delivered today along with pipe. We just have to wait for it, so relax."

Craig looked relieved and Jimmy wondered if he'd been pushing the youngster too hard. "How are you holding up? Am I working you too hard?"

"I'm all right," replied Craig. "I'm not used to getting up so early."

"What time do you usually roll out?"

"Around ten or eleven," answered Craig, "sometimes not until after noon."

"You'll get used to getting up early, it just takes time. You've been falling asleep pretty quickly when you hit the sack, haven't you?"

"I guess so," answered Craig.

"There'll be plenty of work after the sewer system is hooked up," said Jimmy. "I think you'll be plenty tired after we fill in the trenches."

"If you're trying to wear me out, you can't do that," said Craig.

Jimmy noted a little tone of defiance in Craig's voice. He remembered his early days at the Wilson Ranch and wondered if his own defiance was as obvious to Bud, Pat, and Honey as Craig's was to him. There was one difference though, work on the Wilson Ranch had to be done as a matter of course. Was the situation here looking for "make work" projects to keep Craig occupied? He decided that "make work" projects wouldn't do, especially when there would be more youngsters on the ranch. He would have to find other projects that would keep the kids busy and help to improve their attitudes.

Then it occurred to him that the rehabilitation project involved horses! He needed more horses to keep everyone busy. But how could he get them without any money? Remembering his days at the Wilson Ranch, he recalled that a good part of the free time in the winter was involved in halter breaking weaner colts. With a bunch of colts to halter break, he could keep a lot of kids busy. But where could he get some colts?

He pondered the question while he and Craig waited for the truck to arrive.

Craig asked, "When is the truck supposed to be here?"

"Mister Mason said they'd be here early, but it's already past nine. I guess early for some folks isn't as early as it is for others," replied Jimmy. He noticed that Craig was showing some signs of restlessness and decided that he wasn't working Craig too hard. He came to the conclusion that Craig would be better off staying busy.

About ten, the truck showed up with the septic tank. Another truck followed with the pipe.

"I'd have gotten here earlier, but we had a flat," said the driver. "I'd still be changing it if our second truck with the pipe hadn't shown up and helped me. We had to go back to town and get the tire fixed."

"You're here now and that's all that counts," replied Jimmy. He pointed to the piles of dirt that lined the trenches and the hole where the septic tank system was to be installed. "It goes over there."

The driver drove the truck beside the hole. With the hoist on the truck, he placed the tank in the proper position. Jimmy and Craig helped unload the pipe with the driver of the second truck.

"We'll handle this from here on out," said the driver of the first truck. "We want it done right. We'll have to glue each pipe at the joints. It will have to dry overnight and then you can back-fill the whole system. Have you got a tractor?"

"No," replied Jimmy.

"You'll have to back-fill the system by hand. It'll take some time and you'll have to be careful not to throw any big rocks on the pipe itself. Sometimes the big rocks will break the pipe or cause the joints to come undone. We don't want that to happen."

The driver returned to his work and it occurred to Jimmy that they had been dismissed. They weren't needed and couldn't back-fill until tomorrow.

"How's about another horse ride?" asked Jimmy.

"I guess so," answered Craig.

"Let's get something to eat, then saddle our horses. You remember how to saddle?"

"Of course," answered Craig. "Where are we going?"

"I don't know, but we'll stay pretty close to the ranch. I guess this will be a pleasure ride to get you accustomed to riding. Everything we do can be a learning experience for you."

"But I don't want to learn to be a cowboy!" replied Craig.

"That's fine," returned Jimmy. "You don't have to learn to be a cowboy, but what you learn here will help you as you grow up. What do you want to be?"

"I dunno."

"Hopefully you'll learn to accept responsibility, show consideration and compassion for others, and become a useful member of society. I hope what you learn here you'll be able to apply in your grownup life and get along well. We'll see."

Craig stepped into the stirrup and started to get on the horse, but the saddle rolled! Hastily, he stepped off before he fell while Jimmy laughed.

"Old Max is pretty wise," said Jimmy. "He'll suck in a lot of air just before you tighten the cinch. It's good to move him a step or two then recheck your cinch. Then when you get on, spring up into the saddle. Don't pull yourself up like you were lifting weights. If you know how to do it, you can get on a horse without the cinch being done up."

"Really?"

"Yep," he answered and Jimmy showed Craig how to do it.

Craig stood spellbound as Jimmy got on the horse without the cinch.

"It's just a matter of balance, coordination, and timing," said Jimmy.

"Can I try it?"

"I'd put that off until you learn how to get on properly with the cinch tight," said Jimmy.

When Craig mounted successfully, they rode off. As they rode, Jimmy tried to find out what Craig wanted to do with his life. It was plain that Craig didn't have a plan or even an idea of what he wanted to be.

They rode by the hayfield and Jimmy noted that the hay was prime for cutting. He thought a ride to the neighbors would be pertinent, and decided to ride over to the Burkharts next day to see when it would be done.

When they returned to the ranch, the sewer system had been installed and the men had left. After supper, Jimmy contemplated back filling the sewer system first thing in the morning, but decided that a visit with the Burkharts was more pressing. A little longer for the glue holding the pipe together wouldn't hurt.

The next morning after breakfast, Jimmy and Craig saddled their horses and started riding toward the neighbors. Halfway down the road, they met Burkhart driving a tractor with a mowing machine behind it. The farm machinery took up most of the road and Jimmy and Craig had to ride their horses into the ditch to let it by.

Burkhart stopped the tractor alongside the horsemen. "Out for a morning ride?" The question was more of a statement than a question.

"We were riding over to visit you," said Jimmy.

"I ain't got time for visiting," stated Burkhart. "I got to cut your hay."

"That's what we wanted to visit about," replied Jimmy.

Pointing toward Craig, Burkhart asked, "Is that one of your delinquents?" His tone didn't indicate any friendliness.

"He's our hired man," replied Jimmy.

"Looks kinda young to be a hired man. Why ain't he in school?"

"He thinks he'd rather work than go to school."

"Don't he know school's work?"

Craig was getting uncomfortable with the talk about him and not being invited to join in. And it showed.

"He kinda thinks he'd rather work out in the open and for wages," answered Jimmy.

"You paying him?"

"Right now he's working for room and board."

"I hope you get your money's worth out of him," said Burkhart. "This ain't getting your hay cut," he said as he drove away.

"He's a crusty old bas …"

"Watch your language there, Craig. Regardless of what he is, we need him to cut our hay. I was told he was hard to get along with, but he's an honorable man."

"I'll believe that when I see it," responded Craig. "He didn't seem very neighborly."

"Nope, but he's cutting our hay, as agreed. Now we can go back to the ranch and fill in the sewer system. I know you've been looking forward to that!"

"I haven't been looking forward to anything since I've been here, except maybe you doing the cooking," said Craig. "I don't think much of my cooking."

"I'll agree with you there," said Jimmy. "I don't think much of it either!" Craig laughed and Jimmy joined in.

They rode back to the ranch, unsaddled the horses, and turned them loose. The next chore was the back-filling. They found a couple of shovels and began the job.

It was difficult work for Craig and beads of sweat started forming on his forehead. Noticing this, Jimmy called for a break. "Need some water?"

"Yes," answered Craig.

They went to the house and got some water. It was clear to Jimmy that Craig was out of shape.

"I think we'll be done with this tomorrow," said Jimmy.

"Tomorrow won't be soon enough for me," replied Craig.

"You ready to get back to work?"

"Not yet," replied Craig.

"The sooner we get this done, the better off we'll be," said Jimmy. "I've found that sometimes the hardest part of a hard job is getting started. Of course the sooner we get started, the sooner we'll be done."

After a few more minutes, Craig was ready. Jimmy noticed Craig's hands. Blisters were already starting to form on his hands. "Better take these," said Jimmy, as he handed Craig his gloves.

"But you won't have any," said Craig.

"I've got another pair in my saddlebags," said Jimmy, as he headed to the barn.

"Thanks," said Craig.

Jimmy got his gloves and as he went back to the trenches, he thought, *Maybe consideration of others is happening in Craig's case.*

At noon, they broke for a meal.

"I've made one decision already," Craig proudly announced while they were eating.

"What's that?"

"I've decided I don't want to be a ditch digger!"

Jimmy laughed and almost choked on the mouthful of food he had. When he regained his composure, he said, "That's a step in the right direction. But don't be disappointed if there's more shovel work to do. By this time tomorrow, we'll be done."

Craig didn't look pleased. He asked, "How long did it take you to dig all this?"

"It took about half a day," answered Jimmy.

"Half a day? I don't believe it!"

"Well, it's true. Of course it was done with a backhoe."

"A backhoe! Where is it?"

"The guys that did the digging took it with them when they left," answered Jimmy.

"Well, they're not very responsible," stated Craig.

Jimmy laughed again. "It was part of the deal. They donated their time and machinery."

A Change

The sewer system got filled in and the next few days were spent riding around on the National Forest, exploring.

One morning as they were riding out, Burkhart came driving in on his tractor pulling a hay baler. "Your hay is about ready to be baled. I'll get it baled, we'll let it set a couple of days then me and the Missus will be over to haul it. Where do you want it stacked?"

"Over there," said Jimmy, pointing to the barn. "Have you got your hay hauled in?"

"No," answered Burkhart. "We'll do it after I've baled yours."

"We?" queried Jimmy.

"Yeah. Me and the Missus," replied Burkhart.

"Well," said Jimmy, "if you'll let us know when you're ready to do that, Craig and I will come over and help out."

"You'll know as soon as I'm done baling yours," said Burkhart, as he drove off. Burkhart didn't seem too willing to receive any help from anyone.

Jimmy and Craig rode out and Jimmy was struggling with the ways and means to acquire horses. They certainly couldn't buy any. "There's too much to do on the ranch yet," Jimmy said out loud, talking to himself.

"What are you talking about?" Craig hadn't been included in this conversation.

Jimmy, brought out of his private thoughts by Craig's question, answered, "I was just trying to plan what to do and how to do it, without any money or materials."

"What do you mean?"

"We've got to build a bunkhouse, make a fence between the pasture and the hayfield, and build a barn, after we tear down the old one, and build new corrals. In addition to that, we need supplies. Beds and bedding for the bunkhouse, dishes, utensils. And we need a cook. I don't see how it's all going to come together."

"Are you getting discouraged?"

"No," answered Jimmy, "are you concerned?"

"Yes," was Craig's reply.

It was Jimmy's turn to ask questions. "Why?"

Craig looked a little embarrassed. "I kinda like it out here."

Again Jimmy asked, "Why?"

"I dunno. I guess it's because there's something to do most of the time."

Boredom! Jimmy knew boredom was part of the juvenile delinquency problem from his own experience. He decided to pursue this line of questioning.

"You even liked the back-filling?"

"I didn't much care for that," answered Craig, "but it's done and I don't have to do it again."

"Not that we can foresee," interjected Jimmy. "But if we do have to do it again, you'll know how to do it, right?"

"I guess so," answered Craig, somewhat dubiously.

"There's going to be plenty of undesirable jobs around here in the future," said Jimmy. "The sooner we get them done, the sooner we can do the fun stuff. But it all has to be done. As a matter of fact, I'm thinking of a very undesirable job right now."

"What's that?"

"I'm thinking we need to clean the corrals when we get back," answered Jimmy. "We've been kinda lax on that lately."

They rode for a while and returned early to the ranch. After unsaddling the horses, they found some shovels, a wheelbarrow, and a corral that was becoming cluttered with horse manure. They started cleaning corrals.

"Where are we gonna put this stuff?" asked Craig.

"We don't have a truck or a manure spreader, so we'll just pile it outside the corral and move it later," answered Jimmy.

Within an hour they had the corral clean and were starting supper preparations when the phone rang.

"Grab that," Jimmy told Craig, "and answer it Juvenile Rehabilitation Ranch Project."

Craig did as he was told and handed the phone to Jimmy. "It's Mister Mason," he said. Jimmy wiped his hands and took the phone.

"You've got Craig answering the phone," said Mason.

"Yep," replied Jimmy. "It's just one of the many things he's learned out here."

"What else has he learned?"

"He has learned that a shovel needs constant supervision and has to be directed in its every movement," replied Jimmy.

Mason laughed. "What does he think of that?"

"Not much. He's already decided he doesn't want to be a ditch digger when he grows up."

"That might be a step in the right direction," commented Mason. "I take it you've filled in the sewer system?"

"Yep. You'd hardly know there was ever a hole or trench there."

"What I'm calling about," continued Mason "is that tomorrow I'll be coming out with a surprise for you. I'll be out around noon, so stick around."

"A surprise! For me! What is it?"

"If I told you, it wouldn't be a surprise," said Mason. "Just be there."

"Okay. Will you be eating out here?"

"What are you having?"

"At this point in time," replied Jimmy, "it looks like we're having peanut butter and jelly."

"I'll get something in town," said Mason.

The next day, Jimmy and Craig puttered around the ranch doing odd jobs until Mason was scheduled to arrive. At noon, when he hadn't arrived, they ate their noon meal.

"I guess Mister Mason doesn't like peanut butter and jelly," said Jimmy.

"I don't blame him," replied Craig. "I'm getting a little tired of it myself."

"We'll see about going into town and getting some more groceries in the next day or two. Maybe even getting a meal at a café."

"That would be swell!" It appeared that Craig was getting tired of his and Jimmy's cooking.

While Jimmy and Craig were eating, a white pickup truck bearing the seal of the state pulled into the yard followed by another state car and an unmarked car.

"I'll bet that's the most cars that have been on this place at one time in a couple of years," muttered Jimmy, as he went out to find out what was going on. He was surprised to see Mason get out of the car with the state insignia. A young man about Jimmy's age got out of the pickup.

Jimmy thought he recognized the man, but wasn't sure. A woman got out of the unmarked car.

"This is quite a parade," remarked Jimmy, as he shook Mason's hand. "There are more cars here now than there has been in a long time."

"Yes," said Mason, as he shook Jimmy's hand, then Craig's. "How are you getting along Craig?"

"Okay, I guess," answered Craig, somewhat restrained. Although he had loosened up a little around Jimmy, he was still reserved around his probation officer.

"Well, Jimmy, this is your surprise," said Mason, taking Jimmy by the arm to the pickup. "I have managed, by somewhat dubious means, to acquire this truck from the state motor pool to use here on the ranch. It's not ours, but it is ours to use."

"That's fantastic! But you're a day late," said Jimmy. "We just cleaned the corrals yesterday and we could have put the manure in the truck and hauled it off."

"Not before you unloaded it," said Mason. Looking into the back of the truck, Jimmy saw bundles of steel posts and rolls of barbed wire.

"There are forty steel posts there and eight rolls of barbed wire," said Mason, proudly. "Oh, I beg your pardon, I believe you know Mister Williams here."

"Oh, yes!" Jimmy shook Dale Williams' hand and greeted him

warmly. "I didn't recognize you with the moustache. How you been?"

Dale Williams had been the second juvenile delinquent to spend some time at the Wilson Ranch, where this juvenile rehabilitation project was tried out as a result of Bud Wilson wanting to help out Jimmy because he knew Jimmy's father.

Mason didn't give Dale a chance to respond much as he introduced the woman. "This is Emily Rich. She's applied for our cook position."

"She's got the job if she can fix something besides canned beef stew and peanut butter and jelly sandwiches!" interrupted Craig.

"Miss Rich is here on a trial basis," continued Mason after everyone had stopped laughing. "She's to cook for a month and then we'll make a final decision."

"Emily Rich, huh?" said Jimmy, as he stuck out his hand.

"Not really rich," replied Emily, as she shook Jimmy's hand, "just near well to do." Everyone laughed as Jimmy sized up Emily Rich. She was in her late thirties or early forties. The crow's feet around her eyes and the lines on her tanned face made it difficult to guess her age accurately, but they indicated a tough life up to this point. Her hands were tanned and had burn scars on them. She was of medium height, perhaps a few pounds overweight.

Jimmy asked, "Can you cook?"

"Why certainly," replied Emily. "I wasn't sure what you had here, so I brought my own equipment along with some groceries I got at the store. What do you want for supper?"

"Prime rib would be nice," answered Jimmy.

"I don't have that," answered Emily. "How about some pork chops, scalloped potatoes, and corn on the cob?"

"That would be great!" interrupted Craig.

"Good," said Emily. "Help me unload the car and get moved in and I'll start supper. What time do you want to eat?" Turning to Mason and Dale Williams, she added, "Will you gentlemen be joining us?"

"No," replied Mason. "We've got to get back to town. I need to talk to Jimmy."

"Craig," said Jimmy, "put Miss Rich's personal stuff in my office. She can bunk there until we get better established. And show her around the house."

"There's an extra cot in the back of the truck," said Mason. "Get it for Miss Rich."

"Yes sir!" Craig seemed anxious to help.

As Jimmy and Mason were discussing Miss Rich, Richard Burkhart came through the yard driving the tractor and baler. He stopped only long enough to say, "Your hay's baled," and drove on.

"He doesn't seem to be a real social animal," said Jimmy. "I'm planning on taking Craig over there tomorrow and help him haul hay."

"Whatever you say," answered Mason. "As I was saying, Miss Rich is here on a trial basis, keep an eye on her and see how she acts around the teenagers."

"Is she on probation or anything?"

"No, she's got a clean record as near as I can find out. She's cooked before and done hunting camps in the past. I want to know about her interaction among the teenagers. It's very important we hire someone that can be a positive influence out here."

"I see," replied Jimmy. "Where does Dale Williams fit in?"

"He doesn't. He's become a paralegal involved with a law office in town and when he heard that I needed someone to drive the truck out here, he volunteered. You remember him from the Wilson's?"

"Yes, of course. Do Bud and Honey have any juveniles this year?"

"No," answered Mason. "With the implementation of our program here, they have declined to accept any more delinquents."

"That's good," said Jimmy. "They've got plenty to keep them busy as it is."

"Yes," said Mason, "but we owe them a lot."

With Emily's car unloaded, Mason and Dale prepared to return to town.

Mason asked, "You still have a list of what we need?"

"We still need a bunkhouse."

"That's liable to be a problem," replied Mason. "I'll see what I can do, but see what ideas you can come up with to get this accomplished."

At supper, Jimmy explained the purpose of the Juvenile Ranch Rehabilitation Project to Emily. He ended by saying, "We don't have any government funding. Most everything we have has been donated. But we need a lot more. We're always looking for ways to generate some money."

"Why not have a barbeque? They are always good fundraisers," said Emily.

"We have never had the funds to have one or a cook to do it, until now," said Jimmy. "Besides, we're so far out of town, it would be difficult to get people to come. Our big problem now is getting a bunkhouse built."

"A barbeque could help raise money to start on a bunkhouse," replied Emily.

"Right now, we've got to hit the sack. Craig and I are going to help the neighbors haul hay tomorrow."

"Okay," said Emily. "I'll fix you some food to take along. What do you want?"

"Anything but peanut butter and jelly," chimed in Craig, who had been listening.

"What time will you be leaving?"

"We probably won't leave until around eight," answered Jimmy. "But we'll be up a little before six."

"Okay," said Emily. "Breakfast will be ready at quarter after six. Omelets okay?"

"Omelets would be super!" exclaimed Craig.

The next morning after breakfast, Jimmy and Craig drove to the Burkharts. Craig couldn't stop raving about how good the supper had been last night or how "fantastic breakfast was this morning. This is going to be a good summer," he said.

When they got to the Burkharts, Burkhart and his wife were in the hayfield. Jimmy drove the truck to the field. Missus Burkhart was driving the tractor and Burkhart was throwing hay onto a low trailer.

"We thought we might lend you a hand," said Jimmy, as Missus Burkhart stopped the tractor and Jimmy and Craig approached.

Burkhart eyed them suspiciously, climbed on the trailer and said, "You can throw those bales to me. I'll stack them."

"Craig, you go on the other side and throw the bales on the trailer," said Jimmy. "I'll do this side. When you can, throw the bales as near as you can to where they'll be stacked. We'll make this as easy as we can for everybody."

They commenced loading hay. Missus Burkhart slowed the trailer when she saw that Jimmy and Craig were putting more hay on the trailer than her husband could handle, and Jimmy thought that was good. He wouldn't have to trot to keep up.

Before dinner, they took two loads of hay to Burkhart's barn. Missus Burkhart helped unload the first load, stacking it in the barn. Burkhart had a portable elevator and he kept everyone busy loading it with the hay. Missus Burkhart kept right up with Jimmy and Craig, stacking every third bale. Jimmy was surprised at how well Missus Burkhart handled the hay. It was obvious that she'd spent plenty of time in the hayfield. Her hands were tanned and calloused.

But she turned to leave when they started unloading the second load. "Lunch will be ready when you have that unloaded," she said.

"Don't bother fixing anything for us," said Jimmy. "We brought our own dinner."

"Very well," replied Missus Burkhart, "but come to the house and get cleaned up before you eat!"

"Yes ma'am," answered Jimmy.

When they entered the Burkhart's to get cleaned up, Jimmy was surprised at how clean and orderly the house was. Missus Burkhart was a good housekeeper also.

When they had cleaned up, Jimmy said, "We'll eat our dinner out under the tree in the shade."

"You can eat with us," stated Missus Burkhart.

"That's fine," replied Jimmy. "We'll eat out under the tree."

"Well, you take this lemonade and a couple of glasses," said the woman, as she handed a pitcher and two glasses to Craig. "It's cold."

Jimmy and Craig sat out under a shade tree and ate their dinner. Craig remarked, "That Burkhart feller doesn't say much, does he?"

Apparently not," answered Jimmy, thinking that he hadn't said a word, other than a curt "Morning" when they showed up. He hadn't even given instructions when Jimmy and Craig showed up, volunteering to help. "He is kinda quiet."

After dinner, Craig returned the pitcher and glasses to the house. "Be sure and thank Missus Burkhart for the drinks," Jimmy reminded Craig.

"Yes sir!"

Craig returned the glasses and pitcher to the house. When he returned to the shade tree where Jimmy was waiting, he said, "Burkhart says we'll start again in about an hour."

"That's Mister Burkhart to you! We might just as well relax."

Later, Mister and Missus Burkhart emerged from the house. Missus Burkhart came to the shade tree where Jimmy and Craig were waiting. Craig had dozed off.

"We're ready to start again, if you are," she said.

"We're ready," said Jimmy, nudging Craig from his nap.

Missus Burkhart drove the tractor to the hayfield and the men rode on the trailer.

"We'll get three loads this afternoon," said Burkhart. "I've got the evening chores to do. With you two guys here, I'm getting more hay on the trailer each load. You boys will eat supper with us when we're done, won't you?"

"We appreciate the offer," said Jimmy, "but we've got a cook over at our place and she'll have supper ready for us when we get done."

Not another word was said by Burkhart the rest of the afternoon while they hauled and stacked hay. When the third load was completed, Burkhart said, "We, the Missus and I, want to thank you for your help."

"You're welcome," answered Jimmy. "What time do you get started in the morning?"

Burkhart looked surprised. "I generally get my chores done by seven-thirty or eight o'clock."

"Good," replied Jimmy. "We'll be here then. How many days hauling hay do you figure you have?"

"Probably about five or six," replied Burkhart. "Then we've got a couple of days getting yours."

"Good," answered Jimmy.

"If you are coming to help tomorrow, be prepared to eat your noon meal with us," said Missus Burkhart.

"That's not necessary," said Jimmy.

"Oh, yes it is," said Missus Burkhart. "I insist!" Burkhart just shrugged his shoulders.

"If you insist," replied Jimmy.

At the end of the day, Jimmy and Craig returned to their ranch. Emily was waiting for them on the front porch.

"How was your day?" she asked.

"A lot of work," answered Craig. "I'm so hungry, I could eat a horse!"

"That won't be necessary. I have something else all ready. Oh, by the way, Mister Mason called. He said he'd be out day after to-morrow for a visit."

"I'd better call him and tell him to postpone his visit until next week sometime. We've got a few days of hauling hay ahead of us. I'll call him before supper."

Jimmy called Mason. "I was just leaving," said Mason when he answered the phone. "You're lucky you got me."

"Lucky?" replied Jimmy, mockingly.

"Yes," replied Mason. "I was thinking of coming out in a couple of days to see how things were going."

"Better put that idea off for a week," said Jimmy. "We've committed ourselves to hauling hay for the neighbors."

"You're hauling hay for the neighbors! How much are they paying you?"

"They're not paying us anything," replied Jimmy. "This is public relations work. And we'll get our own hay hauled."

"I guess that's good," said Burkhart. "How much hay do you have?"

"Probably around a couple thousand bales. We'll have to see when we figure Burkhart's share. It should be plenty."

"We might want to see if we can sell some of it to raise money," said Mason.

"I don't think we want to sell our feed," replied Jimmy. "It might be better to see how much hay we actually have before we try to sell some."

"But we need money," said Mason.

"We'll have some calves to sell from Missus Grundy's cows, probably only ten head or so. Maybe some cull cows, too. But let's keep our hay until we see what we actually need."

"You're the boss," said Mason. "But even though this is a non-profit operation, we still need to have some money coming in. You need to be thinking of some ways to generate some income. You call me when you get done hauling hay and I'll come out then."

"Okay," replied Jimmy.

After supper that night, Jimmy and Emily sat on the porch visiting. Craig went to bed early, being really tired after a hard day's work.

Jimmy asked, "Do you have any ideas on how we can raise money for this project? Mason seems really concerned about our cash flow. I think we're running out of money."

"I still think putting on a barbeque for a fundraiser is a good idea," replied Emily.

"But that requires a lot of money," stated Jimmy.

"Not so much when you buy the food right," said Emily. "And I can prepare a lot of food cheap! If you sell tickets for admission and set some donation cans out in plain view, you might be surprised what you can raise. Of course you need to publicize the event with some flyers and some newspaper advertising. Let the general public know what you're trying to do out here. And, of course, you need to let people know that you're always willing to accept volunteer work."

"You might have an idea there," replied Jimmy. "But if we get people out here, what do we have to show them? The place is pretty run down."

"That's the beauty of the situation," said Emily. "The place needs improvement and people can see that. Show people where you're going to put the dormitory and …"

"Bunkhouse," interrupted Jimmy. It was clear that Emily had been informed by Mason about the overall plan.

"Bunkhouse, I stand corrected," said Emily. "People can see that we need a barn and corrals. Give people a guided tour and explain what we need. Always keep in mind that we're trying to rehabilitate these young people. Remember, it's all for them."

Jimmy was impressed with Emily. She seemed to take a real interest in the operation and was including herself with the use of the word "we."

"You work things out for the barbeque and discuss them with Mason when he comes out. I still have to figure out how to keep the juveniles busy when we get everything going."

The following days were busy hauling Burkhart's hay. Jimmy and Craig ate their noon meals at the Burkhart's when they were hauling their hay.

When they hauled the Juvenile Ranch Rehabilitation Project's hay, Jimmy invited the Burkharts to eat with them for the noon meal, which they did. It was obvious that Missus Burkhart lacked female companionship, the way she visited with Emily. They seemed to get along well.

Burkhart himself seemed pleased with the help he had gotten from Jimmy and Craig. "We saved about three days with your help," he said. "We'll be able to get started irrigating sooner. The way I've got it figured, you've got more than two thousand bales coming and I've got about a thousand."

"That's more hay to us than I figured," said Jimmy.

"It probably is," replied Burkhart. "But it's close enough. Your help and the youngster's is worth the difference."

Jimmy had decided to stack the hay outside the barn, as it was scheduled to be demolished, just when hadn't been decided. When the ranches' hay had been stacked, they hauled Burkhart's share to his place. While they were stacking the hay, Jimmy explained the ideas behind the project to Burkhart.

Burkhart commented, "You don't really need a big barn. Just build a barn to handle what you need for your livestock. You can build a pole barn for the hay. It's open on all four sides and it's a lot cheaper. It will provide sufficient protection for the hay."

"I hadn't thought of that," said Jimmy. "Thanks for the idea. Let me know when you're ready to haul the second crop and we'll be there to help." Burkhart just shrugged his shoulders.

Jimmy called Mason and asked for him to bring out some big tarps to cover the hay to protect it from the elements. A few days later, Mason arrived with the tarps and Emily immediately cornered him with her idea. Jimmy let Emily guide the discussion with Mason. When she was done, Mason asked Jimmy, "What do you think of this idea?"

"It's worth a try," replied Jimmy. "If it doesn't work, we'll have plenty to eat here."

"Then we'll do it," said Mason. "I'll have the necessary flyers drawn up and printed."

"Don't forget the newspaper," said Emily.

"Right! Now, Jimmy, show me where the structures will be built."

As Jimmy and Mason walked around the farmyard, Jimmy pointed out where the pole barn was to be built, where the corrals were to be built, adding that some separate pens should be built just in case. Alleyways and feeders would have to be built. Stackyards for hay would need to be built also. Mason already knew the location of the bunkhouse.

While they were walking around, Mason asked Jimmy, "How is Emily working out?"

"She is a good cook," replied Jimmy. "And she seems to be taking an interest in the place. I think she's worth keeping, if that's what you're leading up to. I don't know what she's doing while we've been hauling hay, cleaning I suppose."

"That's where I was going," said Mason. "I'll have to talk to her about wages and we're running short of money. You wouldn't mind a delay in your paycheck, would you?"

"I don't really need anything right now, I haven't got any trips to town planned."

"Good! We'll make it up to you. And, I've been thinking, all work and no play for these youngsters won't be good. Where could we put a baseball diamond?"

"I hadn't really thought of that," answered Jimmy. "I guess about anywhere except in the hayfield."

"You seem to be getting along good with your neighbors, the Burkharts."

"I think helping haul the hay has improved his attitude," said Jimmy.

"That was a good move on your part," said Mason.

"I did that because it was necessary," replied Jimmy. "We got our hay hauled, it kept Craig busy for a few days and it showed him, I hope, a lesson in cooperation. I've tried to make everything we do a positive experience for him. I think tomorrow we'll just go for a ride and see if we can find some of Missus Grundy's cows."

"That's good," said Mason. "I'll finalize the barbeque with Emily and we'll go from there. The next project we need to do is the dormitory."

"Bunkhouse," corrected Jimmy.

A New Horse

At breakfast the next morning, Jimmy asked Emily to fix some lunches that they could pack in their saddlebags.

"We're going to look for some cattle and we'll be gone all day. If we had another horse, you could go with us."

"I'd like that," said Emily. "I've done about all the cleaning that's necessary here."

"When we get some more horses, we'll take you with us. But I don't know when that will be."

They saddled the horses and rode out. As they rode, Jimmy decided that tomorrow they'd start building a fence between the pasture and the hayfield.

Entering the forest service property, they took a different trail than the one they had taken before. This was all new range to Jimmy and he thought he'd take advantage of the time and learn the country.

In two hours of riding on the forest they hadn't seen any cattle and Jimmy was becoming concerned about Missus Grundy's cows. Another hour's riding and they saw a lone horseman riding toward them. It was Burkhart.

"Out for a morning ride?"

"We were actually looking for Missus Grundy's cows," replied Jimmy.

"They're all okay," said Burkhart. "I saw them about a mile and a half back, down in a little draw with water. They're with a bunch of my cows. I'll take you to them."

As Burkhart talked, Jimmy sized up his horse. The horse wasn't anything special and was starting to show some age. Burkhart noticed this and said, "Ol' Roany here ain't much anymore. But we manage to get the job done, just a little slower. How you doing, boy?"

Craig was surprised to be noticed by Burkhart. Burkhart hadn't said anything to him all the while they were hauling hay.

"Okay, I guess," stammered Craig. Without thinking, he added, "How are you?"

"Fine," came the curt reply.

"Had your dinner?" asked Jimmy. "We've got some sandwiches we haven't eaten yet."

"I'd be obliged," answered Burkhart.

Jimmy reached into the saddlebag and brought out the lunch Emily had made. "Help yourself."

Burkhart took a sandwich. "We can eat as we ride." He turned his horse toward where he had seen the cattle.

"I understand Missus Grundy has about ten cows," said Jimmy.

"She's got eleven cows and ten calves," said Burkhart. "I had to pull one last spring and lost him. Her cows are getting some age and most of them should be sold."

As Burkhart made his comment, Jimmy thought of Honey at the Wilson Ranch and how hard he'd tried to achieve a hundred percent calf crop and never quite accomplished it. Even on small outfits, there was the chapter on accidents.

"Looks like we'll have at least one cow to sell this fall," said Jimmy.

"You look at Missus Grundy's cows and you'll probably decide to sell more than one," said Burkhart.

As Burkhart ate his sandwich, he threw the waxed paper away. *This wouldn't do at the Wilson Ranch*, thought Jimmy.

"Do you want another sandwich, Mister Burkhart? I've got another one."

Jimmy was surprised that Craig would offer Burkhart another sandwich.

"No, thanks, boy." Burkhart's answer was again curt.

They reached the draw where the cattle were. There were about fifty head there, drinking or chewing their cuds.

"We'll just ride through them real slow and you'll see Missus Grundy's cattle. They're branded with a Bar G on the left rib."

Jimmy saw all of Missus Grundy's cows and determined that about half of them were gummers and would need to be sold in the fall.

"Missus Grundy has permits for about fifty head on the National Forest. She has let me use the permits she hasn't got cows for," volunteered Burkhart.

"That's fine," said Jimmy. "I don't think our Rehabilitation Ranch will be getting more cattle any time soon. We can continue on the same basis until it's time to change."

"Missus Grundy doesn't have a bull; my bulls have been servicing her cows for the last couple of years," continued Burkhart. "You don't have enough cattle to warrant getting a bull for, so we can continue the same way if you want."

"That's fine again," said Jimmy.

"There's a shortcut to your place, if you head off to the west you'll hit a trail that will take you to the edge of your pasture. It'll save you some miles," said Burkhart.

"Thanks," said Jimmy. "We'll take it. Be seeing you soon."

Jimmy turned his horse to the west and Craig followed. "See you later, Mister Burkhart," said Craig as he followed Jimmy.

"Yeah, boy," answered Burkhart. His reply was curt as usual.

Craig trotted his horse beside Jimmy. "That Burkhart isn't much of a conversationalist, is he?"

"Nope," replied Jimmy, "but he's coming around, it'll just take time."

"Well, we got plenty of that," said Craig.

They hadn't ridden very far when they heard some yelling. "What's that?" asked Craig.

"It sounds like Burkhart," answered Jimmy. "Be quiet."

The yelling continued. "Sounds like Burkhart's in trouble," said Jimmy. "We better ride over and see what's happening. You swing off to the left and I'll bear to the right. If you find anything, holler, and holler loud."

They split up and Jimmy was careful to keep Craig in sight

where he could. They headed out at a trot and covered ground quickly.

Presently, Jimmy heard Craig yelling and saw him atop a little rise, waving his arms. Jimmy put Digger into a lope to where Craig was waiting.

"What happened?"

"I found Mister Burkhart down in the draw," answered Craig. "His horse is down and Mister Burkhart has his leg under him. I couldn't get him free."

Craig led the way to where Burkhart was pinned under the horse.

"What happened?" asked Jimmy.

"My horse took a big jump and fell to the ground," said Burkhart. "I couldn't get free so I started hollering, hoping you guys would hear me. I think my ol' horse had a heart attack. He's dead."

"You hurt?"

"I've either broke my ankle or it's sprained pretty bad, I don't know."

"I don't think Craig and I can move the horse," said Jimmy. "If I give you my lariat rope, can you hold onto it? Maybe Digger and I can drag you out from under the horse. It's liable to hurt some."

"I think that's the only option. Let's give it a try," said Burkhart.

Jimmy took his rope off the saddle and tossed it to Burkhart. He turned Digger away from the fallen horse, dallied up and asked, "You ready?"

"Ready as I'll ever be."

"We'll have you out from under that horse in no time," said Jimmy, as he moved Digger away. The horse dug in and slowly Burkhart was dragged out from under the horse. From the way Burkhart gritted his teeth, Jimmy thought it must have been real painful for him, but Burkhart didn't utter a sound.

When he was free from the downed horse, Burkhart sat up and stretched his injured leg. "Broke," he muttered. "Just what I was afraid of."

"Can you ride?"

"If I can get on," said Burkhart.

"Craig," said Jimmy, "you help Mister Burkhart over to that rock. We'll use it as a mounting block to get him on my horse and take him home."

"Yes sir," said Craig.

"It's your left foot that's broken," said Jimmy. "We'll have you get on from the right and take the weight off your left."

"Will that horse load from the right?"

"He should," replied Jimmy, "he's just an old dude horse."

With some struggling, they managed to get Burkhart on Digger and headed off toward the Burkhart ranch.

As they rode, they talked. "If that kid, what did you say his name was?"

"Craig," answered Jimmy.

"Well, if Craig hadn't found me, I don't know what I'd have done. It might have been the last of me. It's a good thing you were out riding today. I'm really grateful to that boy. I'm going to miss my ol' horse, I didn't think coming out here would be too tough on him. We've covered a lot of miles together. I guess when your time comes, it's your time to go." There was a strange sound of regret in Burkhart's voice as he spoke of his horse.

"Some are just luckier than others," replied Jimmy. "If you have another horse we can use as a packhorse, we'll come out and get your saddle tomorrow. I was going to build fence between the hayfield and the pasture tomorrow, but we can do that the next day."

"I've got more horses at the ranch," said Burkhart.

"We'll take your horse home tonight with us and bring your saddle and horse back tomorrow, if that's all right with you," said Jimmy. "We'll probably have to cut the cinch to get the saddle off the dead horse."

"Whatever you want," said Burkhart. "My other horses should follow us right into the corral."

They rode through Burkhart's horse pasture and his horses did follow. Craig opened and closed the wire gates as they rode to the ranch. When they entered the corrals, Burkhart's horses followed and Craig closed the gate behind them.

"Go to the house and get Missus Burkhart," Jimmy told Craig. "Tell her to bring the car to the corrals."

Craig did as he was told and shortly Missus Burkhart arrived with the car. Anxiously, she asked, "What happened?"

"I think I broke my foot," answered Burkhart. "I'll explain on the way to the doctor's. Craig, you go to the barn and get a halter and catch that black horse. While you're there, grab a cinch off one of them other saddles."

Craig did as he was told and Jimmy helped Burkhart to the car. Jimmy asked, "Any chores we can do while you're gone?"

"Turn the horses loose, take some chicken feed to the chickens and fill their water troughs. The Misses can do what's left when we get home. And once again, I thank you. I'm mighty grateful. And a special thanks to you, Craig."

"Yes sir," said Craig.

"Don't mention it," said Jimmy. "Craig, catch the black horse and tie him and ours outside the corral. I'll take care of the chickens."

Missus Burkhart drove off and Jimmy and Craig did the few chores Burkhart indicated. They mounted their horses and rode off, with Craig leading Burkhart's horse.

"Don't get that lead rope under your horse's tail," said Jimmy. "You might end up with an exciting ride."

"Mister Burkhart seems to have softened some," said Craig, as they rode toward their ranch. "He even called me by my name, the first time he's done that. I don't really like being called 'boy'."

"I don't either," said Jimmy as he smiled, remembering his first meeting with Burkhart.

The ride home was uneventful and Craig remarked, "I could do this all day. It's a lot easier than hauling hay or filling in trenches. The horse is doing all the work."

Jimmy asked, "You're getting used to riding?"

"It's getting a lot easier."

"It does become tiresome after a while," remarked Jimmy. "But I will admit that it's easier than hauling hay or filling in trenches."

When they got to the ranch, they found Emily waiting anxiously.

While they took care of their horses, Jimmy told her what happened during the day.

"I've kept supper so warm for so long, I'm afraid it's burnt now," said Emily. "But we'll see what we can salvage."

"I'm sure everything will be all right," said Jimmy.

"Craig," said Emily, "it turns out that you're the real hero of the day!"

"How's that?"

"Didn't you find Mister Burkhart? And didn't you get help?"

"Well, yes," answered Craig.

"Then that means you're a hero. There's no telling what would have happened to him if you hadn't found him," said Emily.

"But I didn't do anything somebody else wouldn't have done," replied Craig.

"But you did it. Heros don't come in fancy costumes. They're all over the place. You just don't recognize them all the time. You're a real hero," said Emily.

"If you say so," said Craig, not fully convinced of his hero status.

After supper, Craig went to bed early and Jimmy and Emily visited on the front porch.

"You laid it on pretty thick to Craig before supper," said Jimmy.

"It was called for," replied Emily.

"How do you figure?"

"These juvenile delinquents all seem to suffer from a feeling of being worthless," answered Emily. "They don't seem to have any self-esteem or self-worth. They seem like they're always getting into trouble trying to be something they're not. When they do something, even when it's wrong, and a lot of the time it is, it gives them something to brag about."

"Laying it on pretty strong like you did to Craig, doesn't that compound the problem?" Jimmy had learned a lot of what Emily was talking about in college, but he pursued this line of conversation just to see how much Emily knew about juvenile delinquents.

"It could compound the problem, as you say, but it needs to be handled in a positive way. Craig has done something good and he should be commended for it. He should be proud of it. We have to teach him some degree of modesty or humility so that he can continue to do positive things which will result in positive results."

"How do you know so much about this?" Jimmy didn't fully know Emily's background.

"Mister Mason told me a lot about what he had envisioned with this project, and I've talked with the psychologist he plans on sending out occasionally."

"A psychologist? I didn't know anything about this," said Jimmy. "Why?"

"Mister Mason wants to have every youngster evaluated periodically to see if the program is working. The evaluations will be done rather discreetly, informally. He's even told me of your previous, shall we say, difficulties?"

"You know that I'm a former juvenile delinquent," stated Jimmy.

"Yes," answered Emily, "as am I."

"You're one too?" said Jimmy.

"Yes, but my record isn't as extensive as yours is, nor some of the youngsters he is trying to get out here," said Emily.

"Jailbirds, that's what we all are! Can any good come from this?"

"Certainly," said Emily. "Who better to teach young delinquents how to be good than a former delinquent themself?"

"That's a good point," said Jimmy. "Tomorrow we've got to go get Burkhart's saddle. Do you want to go?"

"Certainly."

"Can you ride bareback? You'll have to ride bareback on Burkhart's horse till we get to his saddle, then you can ride his saddle back unless we have to cut the cinch. We'll come back to get you in the truck and save you a long walk home. Missus Burkhart could probably use some company anyway."

"That will be good," said Emily.

The next morning Jimmy and Craig saddled their horses and grabbed an extra bridle for the black. They packed the lunch in their saddlebags that Emily had prepared. Emily got on Burkhart's black bareback and they started out to retrieve Burkhart's saddle.

Craig volunteered to let Emily ride his horse with a saddle and he'd ride bareback, but Emily refused. "I know how to ride bareback," she said.

Emily did know how to ride bareback and proved it by holding onto the black's mane when they went uphill.

They arrived where Burkhart's horse had died. They tried to remove the saddle without cutting the cinch, but were unsuccessful.

"We'll have to cut the cinch," said Jimmy. "Then we can pull the saddle out from under the horse the same way we pulled out Burkhart. Do you have that extra cinch, Craig?"

"It's still in my saddlebag," answered Craig.

They cut the cinch and pulled out the saddle from under the horse, with Digger's help. Jimmy attached the cinch to the saddle then saddled the black and Emily got on.

"We can't adjust the stirrups, he's got the stirrup leathers laced all the way," said Jimmy. "You'll just have to ride with your legs dangling."

Emily laughed. "They've been dangling all the way here."

The ride to the Burkhart's was uneventful. When they approached the ranch, they found Mister Burkhart sitting on the porch with his ankle in a cast.

"It's broke," said Jimmy, eyeing the cast.

"Yep," replied Burkhart. Seeing Emily on his black horse, he asked, "How do you like my horse, young lady?"

"He's good," said Emily, "Although he's a little pigeon-toed. The saddle doesn't exactly fit though. Your legs are longer than mine. "

"Yes, he is, but a pigeon-toed horse will never stumble."

Jimmy was surprised that Emily had noticed the horse being pigeon-toed.

Burkhart laughed. "Well, if you like the horse, just ride him home. I won't be able to ride for some time."

"I could do that," answered Emily, "if it's all right with the boss here."

"I suppose it'll be all right," said Jimmy.

"Craig," said Burkhart, "take the black down to the barn and unsaddle him. You'll find another saddle hanging in the barn. It has those adjustable stirrups. Put it on the black. Miss Emily here should be riding a saddle that fits her and the horse."

"Yes sir," said Craig and he took the black to the barn.

Missus Burkhart appeared at the doorway. "Won't you come in and have some lunch with us?" she asked.

"We ate dinner on the way," answered Jimmy. He was somewhat surprised at Missus Burkhart's referral to dinner as "lunch."

"Well then, come in and have some iced tea or lemonade. We haven't had any company for a long time," she replied. "Richard, you make these young people feel at home."

"Yes ma'am," answered Richard. "You can tie your horses over on the fence there, and then come in the house."

Jimmy tied his horse to the fence and Emily tied Craig's horse to the fence. Burkhart was waiting on the porch, supporting himself on crutches. "Just come on in and sit down at the table," he said. "I'll wait here for Craig."

Iced tea and lemonade were served, Craig came to the door and Burkhart let him in. The women visited and Emily explained her plans about the fundraiser barbeque to Missus Burkhart. When she finished, she said, "Of course, you're invited and we really expect to see you there."

Burkhart and Craig visited and Burkhart couldn't thank Craig enough for helping him the day before.

Jimmy felt largely alone while everyone visited and reflected that some changes had taken place in Craig and Burkhart. He thought they were positive changes, changes for the better.

Soon Jimmy said, "We really must be going. We still have chores to do."

"Won't you stay for supper?" queried Missus Burkhart.

"No, thank you," replied Emily. "I have supper in the crockpot and its been cooking all day. If we don't get back soon, it will be overcooked."

"Well," said Missus Burkhart, "I'll see you to the door, No need for you to get up, Richard, I can show these folks to the door."

Burkhart got up and shook hands with Craig and Jimmy. As the three left the house, Missus Burkhart invited them all back "anytime."

As they got on their horses, Jimmy noticed Emily checking the cinch on her horse. He thought, *She's had more horse experience than I'd thought.*

As they rode toward their ranch, Jimmy asked Craig what he and Burkhart had talked about.

"He couldn't stop thanking me for finding him," said Craig. "When I told him that Emily thought I was a hero for finding him and getting Mister McIntyre's help …"

Jimmy interrupted, "It's Jimmy."

"He agreed I was a hero," continued Craig. "It really surprised me. He might not be so bad after all."

"There's a little good in everyone," said Jimmy. "Sometimes it just needs a little nudging to come out."

Construction

The next day as they were loading the truck with the fencing equipment, Emily came to the barn. "Mister Mason is on the phone for you," she said. "He said it's important."

"I better come and talk to him," said Jimmy.

"He said he had good news for you."

"Then I better hurry. Craig, finish loading up this stuff."

When Jimmy picked up the phone, he found Mason waiting impatiently. Mason said, "Where have you been?"

"Were getting ready to build fence. We try to stay busy out here. Emily said you had some good news for me, what is it?"

"Emily's idea about a barbeque is a go. We've set it up for the twelfth of July. We're going to have an old fashioned barn raising!"

"But we don't need a barn right now," said Jimmy. "What we really need is a bunkhouse."

"That's what I mean," countered Mason.

"I don't follow you."

"I convinced a lumber company to supply the framework materials for a new dorm ... ah, that is bunkhouse. Then I went to their competitors and told them that their rivals had donated the framework for the bunkhouse and we needed some rafters for the roof. They agreed to supply the rafters. It looks like we're in business!"

"That's great," replied Jimmy, "but we'll need siding, plumbing fixtures, beds, and everything else."

"Goodness! You're impatient, young man," said Mason. "You know Rome wasn't built in a day."

"I guess I am a little impatient," replied Jimmy. "At least it's a start."

"Correct. Now you need to have Emily get enough groceries to feed a couple of hundred people."

"A couple of hundred! You're setting your sights kinda high, aren't you?"

"I don't think so," said Mason. "We've printed up flyers explaining what we're trying to do and distributed them all over the state. Every juvenile court in the state has gotten them. I've even had a few calls from some of the juvenile court judges and Judge Reynolds has received a few calls from some of his constituents. Some parents of youngsters under my jurisdiction have indicated interest in the project. This whole program is going to fly! We're receiving more interest in this than I expected!"

"I'll have Emily get the necessary groceries. For that many people, we better get hamburger and hot dogs, it'll be cheaper."

"You're right, my boy, you're right!" Jimmy bristled at the term "my boy," but dismissed it due to Mason's enthusiasm.

"Beans are cheap, and corn on the cob is easy. Maybe some watermelon," said Jimmy.

"Right, right. We've only got a couple of weeks to do this, so get started now," said Mason.

"I'll talk to Emily about what we need and have her get on it right away. She'll be pleased to know that her idea is going to be used."

Jimmy told Emily that Mason had accepted her idea and she could start accumulating supplies. She seemed pleased. "Can you handle a couple of hundred people?" Jimmy asked.

"I think I can," replied Emily, "but I might need some help."

"We might be able to get some of Mason's secretaries to come out and help," said Jimmy.

"That would be good. Let me talk to Louise," said Emily.

"Louise? Louise who?"

"That's Missus Burkhart," answered Emily.

"You handle that. Burkhart is kinda tough to deal with," said Jimmy.

"I can handle it."

Jimmy returned to the truck where Craig had loaded the fencing supplies. "It looks like you might get some company," he told Craig.

"How's that?"

Jimmy explained what Mason had told him over the phone.

"So, we're having a party, huh?"

"Yep, you might want to be on your best behavior."

"Not a problem," said Craig, "I'm sorta liking this."

"We'll see how much you like it when we're done building fence."

Craig asked, "What's so hard about that?"

"We've got to build braces, set corner posts and brace them, pound steel posts, and stretch barbed wire. There's a lot to be done. We also need to build a pole fence leading into the corral. There might be some crowding there and we don't want our horses to get torn up."

Jimmy drove the truck to the end of the pasture. "We'll build a brace here," he said, marking a spot on the ground. He marked another spot about eight feet away from the first spot. "Dig two holes for posts here where I've marked the ground. The holes need to be about three feet deep. You can measure it on the shovel handle. I'll go to the other end and dig two holes there. Then we'll stretch wire and start pounding posts."

Jimmy got Craig started then went to the other end of the field and started digging his holes. The digging wasn't hard and he had two holes dug fairly quickly. He returned to Craig to find him struggling with his first posthole. He had encountered some rocks and the digging was difficult.

"Let me show you how to handle that," he said, as he took a five-foot-long steel bar from the truck. He used the bar to loosen the rocks and pulled them from the hole by hand. "I'll finish this one, you start on the other one."

Before long they had the two postholes dug. "Now we'll plant the posts and build a brace."

"Plant the posts," said Craig. "Do you expect them to grow?"

Jimmy laughed. "No, it's just a term. We'll have to tamp the dirt to make sure the posts are solid."

When both posts were solidly set in the ground, Jimmy said, "Now we'll build a brace."

"Why do you need a brace?"

"That's to keep the end post solid. We'll be pulling the wire with the truck and we don't want to pull the post out. We're building a solid foundation. Just like with a man, if you've got a solid foundation, you'll have a solid man."

Jimmy thought and hoped his comparison of the foundation and brace to a man made sense to Craig. If it did, he reasoned, Craig might get a better idea of what he was doing on the ranch and why he was here.

"There's a space between the end post and the other fence," said Craig.

"Yep, we'll put a gate there. You never know when you'll need it." They built the brace and it was solid.

"Now we'll string the wire," said Jimmy, as wrapped the wire around the end post, about eighteen inches above the ground, and secured it. He put the steel bar through the spool of barbed wire. "Ready?"

"I guess so," answered Craig. "What are we doing?"

"We're going to unravel this wire. Take the other end of the bar and we'll start walking. When we get close to the end, we'll stop and build another brace."

As the wire unrolled, it tended to curl. "Keep walking and don't let the wire coil on itself. A kink will bust the wire when we stretch it."

They unrolled the spool and Jimmy set the bar on the wire to keep it from coiling back on itself. "You watch this wire, don't let it go anywhere," he told Craig. "I'll go back and get the truck and we'll build another brace. This is about halfway to the end."

Jimmy walked back to the truck and brought it to where Craig was waiting. "We'll stretch this a little with the truck," he said, as he fastened the wire to the front bumper of the truck. Making sure the wire was in line with the place where he had dug his two holes, he stretched the wire a little.

"Now, walk along the wire and make sure the wire isn't kinked and that it's straight, not hung up on some grass or weeds," he said to Craig, "then come back."

As Craig walked along the wire, Jimmy watched as he occasionally bent over to free the wire from whatever it might have been hung up on. He would occasionally back the truck up to take out the slack. He didn't want the wire as taut as it would eventually be, but he wanted it tight enough to make a straight line.

When Craig returned, Jimmy backed the truck up to make sure the wire was straight. "We need three post holes here," said Jimmy, marking three spots on the ground.

"Why three?" asked Craig.

"We need to brace here from both ends. We'll pull the lower end from here and pull the upper end from the end nearest the barn."

They started digging, with Jimmy digging the center hole. He finished before Craig had finished his hole and started the third one. When Craig got done with his hole, he volunteered to help Jimmy. "I've about got this one," said Jimmy.

"You dig about two holes to my one," said Craig.

"That's true," said Jimmy. "A lot of this is knowing how to do it. You'll learn. Experience is the best teacher."

They built the three-member brace. "Let's walk this off and figure out where to put our steel posts."

Jimmy walked, counting off his carefully measured footsteps. When he got to the end, he wrote down the number of footsteps. Then he asked, "How many steel posts do we have?"

"I dunno," answered Craig. "They're all in the truck."

"We need to count them so we can space them fairly evenly along here. We'll get the truck and measure the distance from the middle brace to the corrals." They walked back to the truck and drove it to the middle brace.

"You count the steel posts while I walk this end off," said Jimmy.

Jimmy walked off the remaining distance, wrote the number of steps down and totaled his figures. He returned to the truck.

"We have fifty-five posts," reported Craig.

Jimmy did the math. "That means we'll need a steel post every forty-one steps," he said. "I'll step off the distance and mark each spot by digging up a little dirt. You come along and put a post by each little hole. Do you know how to drive?"

Craig nodded his head and said, "A little bit."

Jimmy said, "Okay, you can drive the truck to keep from carrying the posts too far."

Jimmy started walking off the distance, counting his footsteps. Every time he got to forty-one steps, he'd take the shovel he carried and dig a small hole. Craig followed, carrying two posts. When he'd laid down his second post, he'd go back to the truck and bring it forward. Jimmy got to the end of this stretch and waited for Craig to arrive. He wasn't long.

"Now, I'll show you how a steel post driver works," said Jimmy. He took a post, put the driver on it, placed the end of the post on the ground, straightened the post and brought the driver down on the top of the post. The post sank into the ground about four or five inches. A few more thrusts and the steel post was set.

"That looks a lot easier than digging postholes," said Craig. "Can I do one?"

"You'll have the opportunity to do every other one," Jimmy said, as he handed the post driver to him. They went to the next post and Craig drove it into the ground.

"That was easy," said Craig, as they walked to the next post. They worked their way back to the middle brace, alternating driving posts.

With the last steel post set in this section of fence, Jimmy got in the truck and tightened the barbed wire. They stapled the wire to the wooden middle post and tied it off. Jimmy was careful to tell Craig to measure a spot on his pants about eighteen inches from the ground to use as a guide to fasten the barbed wire evenly to the steel posts.

Then they each grabbed a bunch of clips that had been supplied with the steel posts and started clipping the barbed wire to the steel posts. Once that was done along the whole section of fence, they decided to take a break for the noon meal.

Emily wasn't present when they arrived at the house, but there was a note on the table that read: "Your dinner is in the crockpot. I've gone to start preparing for our barbeque. Turn off the crockpot when you're done. Lemonade is in the fridge. Be back soon."

After dinner, they got another spool of wire and unrolled it along the fence. They spaced each line of wire above the previous line and they had a fairly even fence. They repeated the whole process five times and had the lower section of fence completed by suppertime.

Emily had returned to the house by the time Jimmy and Craig had finished with the fencing. She asked, "How did the fence building go?"

"It's going," replied Jimmy. "You were gone all day. Did you get anything accomplished?"

"I think I did. I convinced Louise to come and help with the cookout."

"Now it's a cookout, huh?"

"Yes," replied Emily. "To be proper, we need steaks for a barbeque. Now that it's hamburgers and hot dogs, it's a cookout."

"How did you convince Missus Burkhart to come?"

"I didn't really convince her, she volunteered. Even Richard offered to help."

Jimmy asked, "So, it's Richard now? What help can he be on crutches?"

"He can be a lot of help. He's bringing his portable grills."

"Well, we'll need them," said Jimmy. "We've got more fence to build tomorrow. Then we'll need to get some wooden stays and some corral poles. We'll need to go to the forest to do that."

"I'd like to go to the forest when you go. I thought it was very pretty when we went after Richard's saddle," said Emily.

"You can go if you can come back and fix supper," said Jimmy.

"I'll put something in the crockpot," said Emily.

The next day, Jimmy and Craig completed the barbed wire stretch of fence. They still had to build an alleyway to the corral. They'd build the alleyway out of poles they cut on the forest.

The following day, Emily made lunches and they drove to the

forest. They took a couple of axes, a crosscut saw, and a chainsaw and some extra gas that had been in the barn, and set out to get the poles and stays they needed for the alleyway and barbed wire fence. They also took some rope.

"Craig, I'll cut the trees and you come along when they're down and cut off the limbs with an axe. I'll show you how to do it. We'll need trees about five or six inches across. When you get them limbed, drag them down to the truck and load them. Emily, can you use an axe?"

"Certainly," replied Emily. "How do you think I got firewood for all those hunting camps I cooked for?"

"Okay, Emily, you cut down smaller trees that we can use for stays. They need to be about two or three inches across. Both of you be careful. We don't need anyone cutting their foot off! Let's go! And stay behind me and stay alert. I don't want to cut a tree down on anybody!"

Jimmy started cutting lodgepole pine trees that were about the right size to make corral poles. He'd fell the tree then cut the top off at about twenty feet. Craig would come behind him, cut the limbs off with an axe, and then drag the poles to the truck. Emily would chop down smaller trees, limb them and take them to the truck. Occasionally, Jimmy would cut down a smaller tree, limb it and toss it back to Emily.

"This one's in the way," he'd say.

Around noon they stopped for the noon meal. Jimmy asked, "How many poles do we have?"

"About twenty-five," answered Craig.

"How many stays, Emily?"

"I'd guess about forty, I haven't been counting."

"A couple more hours and we'll have enough," said Jimmy. "I'd rather have more than what we need than not enough."

When Jimmy thought they had enough poles, they gathered up all the stays that had been cut, loaded up their equipment, and went back to the ranch.

When they got to the ranch, Jimmy parked the truck by the corrals and said, "We'll leave all this on the truck and work off the truck. There's no sense in handling it twice. It won't be long before we'll be able to turn the horses out on pasture until we need them."

"I'm going to the house and clean up," said Emily. "Supper will be ready in about twenty minutes."

The next day, Jimmy and Craig were busy digging postholes for the alleyway. They needed to dig ten holes, five on each side of the alleyway, Jimmy having decided that the posts were to be about ten feet apart. That would give them fifty feet of alleyway leading into the big corral. If the alley was twelve feet wide, it should eliminate a lot of crowding.

Craig was getting experience digging postholes and when Jimmy noticed him working up a sweat, he suggested a break.

"No," said Craig. "This isn't much fun and the sooner we get done, the sooner we can move onto something funner."

"Funner?"

"Yes," answered Craig. "More fun!"

Jimmy laughed. Perhaps Craig was changing his attitude.

That night after supper, Emily said, "I'd like to go to town tomorrow and start getting things for the cookout."

"Where are we going to keep everything? And the truck isn't unloaded yet."

"I'll take my car and order the hamburger and hot dogs. We can pick them up the day before the cookout. I can bring home the buns, relish, and other fixings and store them in the kitchen. We need an extra water trough to fill with water to keep the watermelon cold. You like watermelon don't you, Jimmy?"

Jimmy thought Emily's remark was in poor taste, even though it was done humorously. He passed it off and answered, "Certainly I like watermelon! You just be sure you get enough!"

Emily laughed. "There'll be plenty," she said.

Jimmy considered Emily's reference to watermelon to be just joking, and thought for a minute, *Perhaps I'm too sensitive about my race.* But he noted that his race didn't seem to matter to Craig, as he hadn't said a word about it since he arrived.

The next day, Jimmy and Craig nailed the poles to the posts

and they had the alleyway. "Nailing the poles up is a lot easier than digging the postholes," said Craig.

"Yep," said Jimmy. "But we've put those posts in pretty solid. We've built a good foundation for our alleyway."

Emily returned from town later in the afternoon with her car loaded with supplies for the cookout. "I could use some help unloading this, fellers," she hollered.

Jimmy and Craig immediately left what they were doing and went to help her. "This won't all fit in the house," said Jimmy.

"We can leave some of it in the car," replied Emily, "we'll have to. I don't need the car anyway. You guys can go to town and get the meat. Pick up some big coolers to keep the meat in so it won't spoil."

On the tenth of July, an oversized truck and trailer pulled into the yard. The trailer was loaded with lumber. The driver of the truck said, "I'm Chuck Johnson, owner of the Johnson Lumber Company. This is the lumber for the frame to your dormitory."

"Bunkhouse," corrected Jimmy. "The foundation is poured and sits over there. The plumbing is set, don't bust or bend it." Jimmy pointed to where the foundation had been poured. "Park the truck where it'll be easy to unload it."

"I've got a couple of camp trailers coming, where do you want them?"

"Anywhere they won't be in the way," replied Jimmy.

"I've also got a lift coming, where do you want it?"

"As close to your trailer as you can get it," answered Jimmy.

Jimmy got to thinking that he might need to make a parking area to accommodate all the cars that might be coming and to rope off an area under the shade trees to do the cooking. He got Emily and told her to rope off the cooking area before someone parked a trailer there.

The following day another truck arrived with escort cars in front and back of it. There was a sign on the front that said "WIDE LOAD." This truck carried pre-made rafters. The driver got out and introduced himself to Jimmy.

"I'm Roger Johnson, owner of the Certified Lumber Company," he said, as he shook Jimmy's hand.

Jimmy noticed a resemblance between the two men. "Are you guys related?"

"Yes, we're brothers," said Chuck, "although I don't brag about it much."

"You should," said Roger. "Don't you realize how good looking you are? You look just like me!"

"You know," said Chuck, "your comments and personality are just one of the reasons I was born first. I couldn't have taken much more."

"I was only eight minutes behind you, I didn't want you to miss me or get lonely," said Roger.

"Ha! Fat chance!" retorted Chuck.

Jimmy couldn't tell if the implied animosity between the two men was real or just joking, after all, they were competitors, but decided not to pursue the matter.

"How long do you figure it will take to put up the frame and rafters?" Jimmy was anxious to get started.

"With the lift we should be able to put the frame up by noon. It's not that big of a building. Then we can put the rafters on. We should have it ready to stand alone by tomorrow night, or first thing the next day."

"Is there anything I can do to help?"

"No," replied Chuck. "We have our own crews coming. They'll just need a place to park their camp trailers."

Emily approached the men. "If you don't need Jimmy, I can use him, starting right now," she said.

"What do you have in mind for me?"

"Right now," said Emily, "you can put the watermelon in the water trough to get them cold. Then first thing tomorrow morning, you need to go to town to pick up the hamburgers and hot dogs. Be sure and get some coolers with ice to keep the meat cold."

Jimmy asked, "How many people are you expecting?"

"Mister Mason said he thought around two hundred people

were going to show up. Then we have the construction crews, Mister Mason's staff, and us, of course."

"Can you cook for that many people? That's quite a few," said Jimmy.

"I can handle it," replied Emily. "Richard and Louise are coming to help."

"What can they do?"

"We'll find out," answered Emily.

Picnic or Barbeque?

The next day Jimmy and Craig went to town to pick up the meat. He was surprised when he returned to the ranch; there were cars and trailers parked all over the place. The bunkhouse was already framed.

"Those guys work fast. It's going to be a crowded weekend," said Jimmy. "The bunkhouse is framed; all we need are the rafters and siding, and indoor plumbing fixtures, beds, bedding, and furniture. That's a lot, but we're a lot closer than we were."

Richard Burkhart had shown up with his grills and a few portable tables. He'd set them up in the shade under the trees in front of the house.

"What time does this thing start tomorrow?" he asked.

"We're scheduled to start at ten in the morning," replied Emily.

"Then I'll be here at nine," said Burkhart.

Jimmy took care of the chores that evening while Craig helped Emily.

The next morning Jimmy and Craig took care of the chores. Burkhart showed up and started his grills. Missus Burkhart went into the house and started to help Emily prepare for the day.

"Can you cook, boy?"

Jimmy thought Burkhart was referring to him and bristled somewhat at the reference, but relaxed when he realized Burkhart was talking to Craig.

"No sir," answered Craig.

"Well, you help me and you'll learn how," said Burkhart.

Around nine, Mister Mason showed up. His staff followed him in their private cars.

"What can I do to help, Jimmy?" Mason was dressed in his jeans and ready to go to work.

"We'll need somebody to direct the parking," said Jimmy. "And keep the cars out of the hayfield and out of the way of the guys putting up the rafters on the bunkhouse. Barring any unforeseen accidents, the bunkhouse will be ready to stand alone this afternoon, I think. I don't really know how long it's going to take the guys. I've left them alone to do their job. You might have some of your staff keep the visitors out of the construction area, for safety sake."

Mason asked, "What are you going to do?"

"I don't know," answered Jimmy. "I thought I'd kinda wander around and do what needs to be done."

"Good, I've got a job for you." Mason opened the back door to his car and pulled out eight three-pound coffee cans. Each can was wrapped with white paper and stenciled with "DONATIONS." Jimmy took the cans and eyed the lettering suspiciously.

"What are we doing with these? Have we become beggars?"

"No," answered Mason. "However, if people are inclined to want to help out, we should make every effort to accommodate them."

"Where will we put them?"

"They'll be put on the picnic tables."

"Picnic tables? We don't have any," said Jimmy.

"They're coming," said Mason. Shortly, a two-ton truck arrived with eight picnic tables.

"I'll see if we can get the hoist operator to unload the tables," said Jimmy. "We'll set them up under the tree, close to the cooks."

With that done, Jimmy didn't have much to do until Mason came to him with some large posters. The posters had lettering on them, each one was different. One was lettered with "BUNK-HOUSE," another with "POLE BARN FOR HAY STORAGE," and another with "CORRALS."

"Put these where they belong, Jimmy, to give people an idea of what we're going to have and where it will be. You'll probably end up giving guided tours to those people that are interested."

Jimmy got some steel posts and wire. He drove the posts in front of where each structure was to be built and fastened the posters to the posts. With that done, he noticed some cars approaching.

"Our visitors are arriving," he said. He really didn't know what to expect.

The first car to arrive contained Judge Reynolds. "What can I do to help?"

Jimmy almost didn't recognize the judge without his judicial robe. He looked different in his jeans and an old, battered cowboy hat.

"Well sir," said Jimmy, "this is sort of a detention center. I'm not sure you belong here. There really isn't much you can do. You might stick around and tell other people what we're trying to do."

"You're very funny, Jimmy McIntyre. We'll see how funny you are if you show up in my court with charges against you." The judge was smiling when he said that and Jimmy had a good laugh.

"I don't think that will be the case in the future," said Jimmy.

"I hope not," replied the judge. The judge left and walked around looking at things as if he was doing an inspection tour.

Cars started arriving and Mason's staff did a good job of parking the automobiles out of the way.

Jimmy soon found himself giving guided tours and answering questions such as, "What is going to go here?" and "What is that for?" As he answered the questions, he remembered taking out the tourists on the Wilson Ranch and doing the same sort of thing. *On the Wilson Ranch,* he thought, *at least I could ride a horse around while I did this.* He found himself giving walking tours around the ranch grounds.

On one such tour, he grabbed a hamburger from Mister Burkhart, doctored it up with the necessary fixings of catsup, mustard, onions and the like, and grabbed a can of pop from Craig.

When he grabbed the pop, Craig hollered, "Hey, we're charging for them!"

"That's good," said Jimmy. "Charge it to me! We'll square up later!"

During a break in the afternoon, Jimmy found Mason sitting in the shade under a tree. He grabbed another pop and joined him.

"Taking a break, huh?" said Mason.

"Yep. I feel like I've walked a hundred miles and answered a thousand questions. Thankfully, most of the questions were the same, so I knew the answers. I should have made a tape recording."

Jimmy hadn't noticed but Mason was sitting next to a younger man who just seemed to be taking in all the activities. Jimmy studied the man. He was very pale, apparently he didn't get out in the sun much. He was well built and Jimmy thought he probably stayed in shape by working out in a gym somewhere.

"Jimmy," said Mason, "this is Doctor Peterson, the psychologist who's going to be working with you and our clients."

"You might disagree with me, but I really don't need a psychologist," replied Jimmy.

Doctor Peterson laughed. "Obviously you've heard the old joke that 'anybody who needs to see a psychologist ought to have his head examined.'"

"I've never heard that one," said Jimmy. "But I think I can agree with it. How are you going to work with these youngsters?"

"I'm not really going to work with them," replied the doctor.

"That's a shame," said Jimmy. "We can always use some extra help out here."

"Sometimes I wish I could be out in a place like this more often. But I'll interview your prospective clients and be involved in the decision as to when they'll be sent out here. Then I'll come out periodically and interview, actually visit with them, and make an evaluation as to whether or not they're making progress."

"What if they're not making progress?"

"I'll visit with you before I make any recommendations. You'll be very much involved in the process," replied the doctor. "The final decisions will be made by Mister Mason, based on our reports to him."

"That's correct," interjected Mason. "I want this project to succeed and it will take a very negative report before we remove a youngster for disciplinary reasons."

Jimmy asked, "If you remove a youngster, where will he be sent?"

"If he fails here, he will be sent to reform school," answered Mason.

"So this is the last house on the block," said Jimmy.

"That pretty well sums it up," said Mason. "Look! It appears the rafters are done. I'll go over and tell Emily to feed the construction crew for free." Mason left, carefully checking the donation cans as he passed the tables. He seemed satisfied.

The doctor asked, "How do you feel about making decisions that might affect a person for the rest of their life? This is a pretty serious aspect of your job."

"I suppose any decisions I make regarding these youngsters will be based on their own actions," replied Jimmy. "I will try and steer their actions in a positive direction, but I can't be responsible for their actions."

"That's the answer I wanted to hear," said the doctor. "We'll just have to handle this as it goes. However, I want to hear about any destructive behavior—any fights or bullying."

Mason returned. "Emily has taken in a lot of money selling the food, and the donation cans seem to have a lot of cash in them, small change mostly, I suspect. This little venture seems to be doing all right."

"That's good," said Jimmy. "Maybe this deal will work. Looks like all we need for the bunkhouse is the sides, roof, indoor fixtures, electricity, beds, bedding, plumbing and the like. I think we've about got this almost done."

"I think you're being somewhat premature," said Mason. "We've still got a long way to go."

"Yeah," said Jimmy, "but we're a lot closer than we were a week ago. By the way, have you seen Missus Grundy? I haven't seen her and I really expected her to show up. You know, without her, none of this would have been possible."

"She told me she was planning on coming out," said Mason. "But she did say she might be late and wouldn't stay long once she got here."

Missus Grundy did show up toward the end of the day, when some of the visitors were leaving. She was old and frail and Jimmy wondered if this might be the last time he saw her alive. Upon her arrival, she immediately sought out Jimmy.

"Well, young man, it appears like you've got a lot accomplished since I was here last," she said. "You're to be congratulated. I don't hardly recognize the place.

"Here," she said, reaching into her purse, pulling out an envelope, and handing it to Jimmy. "I want you to have this. It's yours to do with as you please. But don't open it until after I leave. Now, give me a tour of what you have done and what you are planning to do."

"It will be a pleasure," replied Jimmy, putting the envelope in his pocket.

The two of them started out on a more detailed tour of the facility than Jimmy had conducted before. He found Missus Grundy to be quite pleasant and she filled him in on some of the history of the ranch. She showed a great deal of interest in what had been done and even more in what was planned for the future.

"When do you plan on putting youngsters in here?"

"We're a long way away from that," replied Jimmy. "But we already have one youngster here, Craig. You saw him when you got something to eat. The frame for the bunkhouse is done, but we need siding, a roof, and all the indoor fixtures. We'll need to pretty well have it complete before we take in any more youngsters."

"Well, do it right, young man, and take your time," said Missus Grundy. "It's better to do it right the first time than have to go back and do it all over."

"I agree with that," said Jimmy, "although Mister Mason can get a little impatient at times."

"I can handle that," said Missus Grundy. "He's a piece of cake."

Jimmy gave the old lady a funny look when she said that, but didn't say anything. Secretly he thought the old gal had a lot of spunk.

"I'd best be going," said Missus Grundy. "I'll speak with Mason before I go. I might want to talk to your young criminal before I go."

"You mean Craig. He's not a young criminal. He's a juvenile delinquent," corrected Jimmy.

"You're right," replied Missus Grundy. "I said that purposely just to test you."

"Test me?"

"Yes. It's important that we have the right people here. You passed my little test satisfactorily by referring to your prospective clients as juvenile delinquents rather than young criminals, as I had called them. You'll do all right here. These youngsters need someone that will stand up for them. Where's Mason?"

"We'll go find him," replied Jimmy.

They found Mason in the house. He'd gathered up some of the donation cans and was counting money. He greeted Missus Grundy courteously as he made some notes on a piece of paper.

"This little venture appears to be showing a profit," he said. "What do you think of our project, Missus Grundy?"

"You appear to be making some progress, however it seems to be moving rather slowly," replied the old lady, as she dropped an envelope on the table where Mason was counting money. "Maybe this will speed things up a bit."

Mason set the envelope, unopened, on a stack of bills that he'd counted. "You need to remember that there are essentially only two of us working on this project, Jimmy and myself. And we're relying heavily on donations of money and materials and labor."

"You take that envelope and go out and buy a lot of what you need—sinks, toilets, and the like—so you can get your dormitory completed."

"Bunkhouse," corrected Mason.

"Bunkhouse, it is," replied Missus Grundy. "But it needs to be done. There are plenty of youngsters that are in dire need of this rehabilitation and they need a decent place to change their lives around."

"It sounds like you've been talking to Judge Reynolds," said Mason.

"I have been and he's very much in agreement with me. As you're probably aware, his juvenile court is overloaded and your own caseload is strained. You could probably use another probation officer in your office."

"That's true," replied Mason, suddenly looking overwhelmed. "However, we're doing what we can, when we can. Relying on volunteer labor is a slow process. Sometimes the volunteers can't finish what they've started and the job has to be put on hold until they find the time to come out and complete it."

"I would suggest that you complete your bunkhouse, make it livable, and then expand the kitchen here in the house, with a bigger pantry, so you can buy groceries on a large scale and save money. And you might want to add another bedroom for your cook. By the way, I've heard a lot about her, I'd like to meet her. What is her name, Richardson, or what?"

"Miss Rich," interrupted Jimmy, "you're confusing her with Craig Richardson. I'll get her for you. She should be able to leave, the day's activities are winding down and a lot of the visitors are leaving." Jimmy left to bring Emily to Missus Grundy.

Missus Grundy and Mason visited while Jimmy was gone.

"Don't misunderstand me, Mister Mason," said the old lady. "I'm very pleased with the progress that has been done here. But there is still so much to do, and I'd like to see it done before I pass."

"I understand," Mason said. "We are making progress, but it has been very slow. However, we're not giving up on this project, it just takes time."

Jimmy returned with Emily. Her hair was a mess and her apron was very soiled. Introductions were made and Missus Grundy said, "My goodness! You look like you're the only one that's been working here!"

"I probably am," answered Emily, smiling. "There's a lot more to putting on these things than meets the eye. I hope you'll excuse my appearance, I have been busy."

"Certainly, I understand that. I'd like to talk to you about this idea. Let's take a walk."

Jimmy excused himself by saying, "I need to get back to work at not working. It's important that I continue, although I feel like I've walked a thousand miles today." Everyone laughed.

Mason said, "And I need to finish counting this money."

Doctor Peterson found Jimmy. "I've got to be going. However, I want you to look for certain behaviors in these youngsters and make notes about them for my evaluations."

Jimmy asked, "What behaviors are those?"

"We want you to look for destructive behavior, fights, anger, and defiance, lack of self-confidence or lack of trust. Any negative action. Make notes on these behaviors."

"You want me to spy on these youngsters?"

"Not spy, just observe. Make notes and give them to me. I'll use them in my evaluations," said Doctor Peterson.

"I would guess that my notes would be mostly negative," said Jimmy.

"Probably," replied the doctor. "However I also want you to look for the positive. As time passes, I would guess the negative comments would diminish and the positive comments would increase. I'll use your comments in formulating my decisions."

Jimmy asked, "I'm going to be the final judge?"

"No, but your comments will be given consideration. I'll check in with you once a month or so when I come out to talk to the youngsters. You might draw up some comments on Craig just to see if you've got the idea."

"I can give that to you now," said Jimmy.

"Go ahead."

"Well, when he first got here he was quiet, sullen, and withdrawn. He appeared to be quite negative. He didn't show a lot of interest in anything, except perhaps the horses. I took him riding, looking for Missus Grundy's cows and learning the country. He wasn't a rider, but warmed up to it. He also worked right alongside me, hauling Burkhart's and our own hay. We also built fence and did other odd jobs as needed. Over time he loosened up and seemed to relax some. I feel like he's come a long way in a short period of time. I can't say how far he's got to go yet, although he appears to be more positive overall now."

"That's what I'm looking for. You're on the right track. I'll make the final evaluation."

The doctor left. Jimmy found a shady spot and settled down for a minute with a slice of watermelon.

The Johnson brothers found Jimmy and joined him. "Our

109

crews have put in some good time and they'd like to camp here tonight and pull out in the morning. Is that all right with you?"

"Sure," said Jimmy. "I don't know that we can feed them in the morning, other than making some coffee."

"They'll be all right," said Roger Johnson.

Emily approached. "Did I hear something about someone staying over?"

"Yes ma'am," said Chuck Johnson.

"Some of the visitors have also indicated a desire to stay longer," said Emily. "I told them to talk to you, Jimmy."

"Nobody has said anything to me," volunteered Jimmy.

"If you let them stay, we could have a pancake breakfast in the morning, for a fee of course," said Emily. "I've got plenty of pancake mix."

"We can do that, if you announce it," said Jimmy. "A lot of the people have already left. But some have set up tents already and some have camp trailers. It looks like it's already a done deal. What are you going to charge?"

"It won't be much. Pancake mix is pretty cheap, and it's easy."

Mason approached, looking very pleased. "We've taken in a lot of money on this little deal. I think there's more people interested in juvenile delinquents than we thought. Now that I've got you Johnson boys together, I think we've got enough money to start putting up the siding and roof on the bunkhouse. Would you boys be interested in submitting a bid to do that?"

"When would you want it done? I've got some other commitments," said Chuck.

"Your crews are already here," replied Mason. "You could start on it as soon as you get the materials. I'd like to get it done as soon as possible."

"Have you figured doors and windows and insulation? What about floors? They all need to be taken into consideration," said Roger.

"Not really," replied Mason. "But I do have the blueprints. You can work off of them, couldn't you?"

Both Chuck and Roger gave Mason a funny look. "We generally use blueprints, but now and then we just play it by ear," said Roger. "Let's see the plans."

"Come this way, fellas, I've got the plans in my car." Mason and the Johnson brothers walked toward Mason's car.

"I'll sure be glad when all this construction is done," said Jimmy. "It seems like that's all that's on Mason's mind."

"Yes," said Emily. "But when the construction's done, that's when your work will begin."

Jimmy asked, "You don't think I'm busy enough now?"

"Oh yes," replied Emily. "But when the youngsters start showing up you might find you've got more than you bargained for."

"We'll see," said Jimmy, "we'll see."

A Pleasant Surprise

The barbeque or picnic was over. Jimmy found himself strangely relieved that the affair was done, he hadn't known what to expect. According to Mason, the event was a success and he was pleased he had convinced the Johnson brothers to put the roof on and get the sides on. Roger was to do the labor and Chuck would send out the materials the next day.

That Mason is quite a conniver, thought Jimmy, as he started to undress for bed. When he took off his shirt, he found the envelope Missus Grundy had given him. He sat down on the bed and opened it up. Suddenly, he jumped up from the bed and shouted, "HOLY MACKEREL!"

Inside the envelope were ten one-hundred dollar bills.

Emily came to his door and knocked. "Are you all right?"

"Come in," said Jimmy.

"What's the matter?" Craig had appeared in the doorway when Jimmy shouted.

"Nothing's the matter," replied Jimmy. "Missus Grundy has given us a thousand dollars! I can't believe it!"

"The old gal must have more money than she needs," said Craig.

Emily gave Craig a disapproving look and asked, "What are you going to do with it?"

"I don't know," answered Jimmy. "She said to use it as I saw fit."

"Well," said Emily, "we can use some more groceries although we still have some hamburger left."

"Make out a list," said Jimmy. "I'll go to town tomorrow and deposit this in the bank and get whatever groceries you want.

This is quite a surprise. I suppose Missus Grundy really believes in this idea."

"She better," said Emily, "she donated all this property."

"I suppose Mason doesn't know about this. We'll just keep it quiet and get stuff we need to operate the ranch as a ranch ought to be operated. We'll be needing some more saddles, bridles, and the like. We'll also need some grain for the horses. We can put this to good use."

The next morning after Emily made breakfast for those people that stayed over and the Johnson brothers' hired men, Jimmy, Emily, and Craig went to town. On the way they passed the Johnsons' trucks headed back to the ranch with the siding and roofing for the bunkhouse.

"They left last night and must have loaded early this morning," said Jimmy.

Craig asked, "Doesn't somebody need to be at the ranch to tell them what to do?"

"No," replied Jimmy. "Those guys already know what to do, and they're pretty good at it. Besides, part of their crew is still at the ranch. They're liable to have it all done by the time we get back."

Jimmy asked Emily, "What did you charge for breakfast this morning?"

"I didn't charge anything, I made it by donation. We've got another fifty or a hundred dollars, I haven't counted it yet."

"Good. We can use it for groceries," said Jimmy.

They made the bank deposit and Jimmy kept back money for groceries and grain for the horses. After the grocery shopping was done they decided to get dinner, although it was early. Much to Craig and Emily's surprise, Jimmy ordered a banana split for his noon meal.

"Why?" Craig and Emily asked almost in unison.

"We've been pretty busy and I thought I'd treat myself," Jimmy replied.

"Good idea," said Craig and he promptly changed his order. Emily did the same, although the waitress gave them all a funny look. It was a little early for ice cream.

"You know, we're acting just like a bunch of teenage kids," said Emily.

"That's all right," said Craig. "I am one!" They laughed and enjoyed a lunch of ice cream.

The trip back to the ranch was uneventful. When they arrived, they found the Johnson brothers' crews busy with the construction. They were a long way from completion.

After unloading the groceries and putting the grain in the barn, Jimmy said, "I think we'll let the construction crews work by themselves. They don't need our help. Our fencing is done and tomorrow, after we do our morning chores, we'll saddle our horses and go check our cows. I feel like I need some saddle time."

"I'd like to go with you," said Emily.

"That's fine," said Jimmy. "Better fix us something to eat before we go."

The next morning, the three of them rode out from the ranch to check the cattle.

"We'd better look at Burkhart's cattle, too," said Jimmy. "He's laid up and probably can't get horseback. I don't know how many cows he's got, but we better look at all we can. He was a lot of help at our cookout."

It was a pleasant ride that morning. It wasn't too cool or too hot, but it was bound to get hotter as the day wore on. Conversation between the three riders was sparse; it seemed like they'd talked themselves out during the cookout. Jimmy had some recurring thoughts about how he was going to keep his clients, the juvenile delinquents, busy when they arrived. The judge and Mister Mason were pushing to get the construction done so they could start sending youngsters out.

In his mind, Jimmy got to wondering when the youngsters would start arriving. It certainly wouldn't be before the bunkhouse was completed. The bunkhouse needed the plumbing and a heater installed. They'd need insulation for the bunkhouse also. Then they'd need to get beds and bedding and some chests of drawers. After all that was done, they'd be ready to start accepting "clients" and start them on the road to rehabilitation. But how?

Jimmy knew that the best way to begin the rehabilitation process was to keep the youngsters busy and busy in a positive manner, but he didn't have enough work to keep a bunch of youngsters busy. As they rode, these questions and problems filled Jimmy's mind. He was watching the country, but not really seeing.

Emily brought him out of his trance when she asked, "What's that dust over there?"

Jimmy suddenly sat upright in the saddle. "It's moving too fast to be cattle and it's headed east. We'll head southeast and see if we can intercept it. It's got to be a truck and we need to see what whoever's driving it is up to."

They picked up the pace to a stiff trot. Craig had a little bit of a problem staying in the saddle until Jimmy told him, "Stand up in the stirrups, it'll be easier on you! You can hold onto the horn." Craig hadn't done much riding faster than a walk.

Soon they reached an old road and waited until the truck approached. They were surprised to find that it wasn't a truck, but a four-wheeler and Richard Burkhart was driving. Missus Burkhart accompanied him. Burkhart stopped the vehicle where the riders were waiting and a cloud of dust enveloped them.

When the dust cleared, Jimmy asked, "Taking the Missus out for a morning drive?"

"Not exactly," replied Burkhart. "It's been a while since I've checked my cows and I thought today would be a good time to do it. What are you doing out here?"

"Same thing," answered Jimmy. "It's a good day to do it."

"That's right," answered Burkhart. "Was your cookout a success?"

"Very much so," said Jimmy.

Emily and Missus Burkhart had started talking and Craig was largely left out of the conversation until Burkhart asked, "How do you feel about the cookout, son?"

"I guess okay, Mister Burkhart," replied Craig.

"You were certainly a big help to me," said Burkhart, "I couldn't have done it without you!"

Interrupting Emily and Louise's conversation, Burkhart asked, "How are you doing with the black horse, young lady?"

"Just fine, I suppose. But I don't have much of an opportunity to use him as much as he ought to be used," replied Emily.

"Well, you just keep him and use him when you need to. He'll be all right." Turning to Jimmy, Burkhart continued, "I'm going to start cutting my hay next week and when I'm done, I'll start on yours."

Jimmy asked, "Is there anything we can do to help?"

"Not until it needs to be hauled. I could use some help then. You guys really made it easy when it came time to haul in the first cutting."

"You let us know when you want to start hauling and we'll be there," said Jimmy.

Burkhart asked, "When are your other delinquents going to show up?"

Craig shot Burkhart a dirty look at his question and Jimmy, noticing this, answered, "It will be some time before our clients start arriving. Our bunkhouse still needs a lot of work done." Jimmy stressed the word "clients."

Burkhart said, "I see," catching on to Jimmy's referral to clients.

Changing the subject, Burkhart said, "I've seen most of the cattle and they're all right. This four-wheeler travels a lot faster than a horse."

"The way you drive," said Missus Burkhart, "this four-wheeler travels a lot faster than most vehicles."

"I'll admit my foot is a little heavy on the gas pedal," said Burkhart, "but this cast doesn't make things any easier. Besides that, you kinda like going fast, don't you, Missus B?"

"Not when you're driving! This thing makes so much noise you can't even hear me telling you to slow down!"

Burkhart smiled and winked at Jimmy. "Speed does have some advantages!"

Burkhart told Jimmy where he'd been and suggested they ride off to the south. They might see some cattle that Burkhart hadn't seen.

"We'll do that," said Jimmy, as he turned his horse to leave. Craig and Emily turned their horses to follow.

They made a big circle and didn't notice anything amiss. They returned to the ranch house to find more vehicles there. There were a few two-ton trucks with lettering on the doors that read, "Simpson Furniture," "DeLong Plumbing" and "Maxwell Siding, Insulation and Doors."

Jimmy looked over the vehicles and decided that Mister Mason had decided to rush the completion of the bunkhouse. They must have made more money than he thought if Mason had bought all this. If all these trucks had what they needed, the bunkhouse would be completed within a week.

The three of them took care of their horses. Emily went to the house to fix supper, Jimmy and Craig went and talked to the delivery people. As near as he could figure, they had about all they needed. The delivery people were also the installers of their goods.

One of the drivers, as he was talking to Jimmy said, "Mister Mason said you folks could feed us until we got the job done. He something about leftover barbeque or something."

"I think we can do that," said Jimmy. "How many people are there?"

They made a quick count and there were twelve. "Craig, go tell Emily to fix extra, enough for at least twelve more."

"How long will it take everybody to put in their stuff?" Jimmy asked.

"If we don't get in each other's way, we should be done in three or four days. There are so many of us here, we might be kind of a bother."

"I'll tell you what," said Jimmy. "Let's get Chuck or Roger Johnson to supervise everyone. I'll suggest that at suppertime. It might help."

"That's a good idea. I think everyone here knows them and they should get along well. I know them pretty well and have worked with them in the past."

"By the way," asked Jimmy, "who are you and what's your crew?"

"I'm Mitch, the electrician. I'm my own crew."

"Very well, Mitch," said Jimmy.

Busy Work

At supper that night, Jimmy outlined his plan. The only objections came from the Johnson brothers. Neither of them really wanted to oversee the operations. Roger finally convinced Chuck that he should do it because he was better looking. They were identical twins and Jimmy couldn't tell the difference. When that matter was settled, Jimmy informed Emily and Craig that he would be gone for a few days.

"Where are you going?" asked Emily.

"I'm going to the Wilson Ranch. We're going to have more clients here sooner than we expected and I think I've found a way to keep them busy. I'll stop in town and tell Mason what I'm doing on the way. If anything comes up, handle it or call Mason. Craig, you take care of the outside chores and help Emily when she asks you."

If the truth were known, Jimmy didn't really want to be around while all the work was being done on the bunkhouse. He didn't feel comfortable as a handyman's helper.

While they had been riding, he was thinking about what kind of programs he could start to help rehabilitate the new clients. There were enough of Missus Grundy's cattle that they could keep a calf back for each youngster and make 4-H or FFA projects. But, they would need more than a calf for each youngster.

Then he thought of the Wilson Ranch. A good part of his winter job had been halter-breaking the weaner colts when he worked for Bud and Honey. Perhaps he could convince them to let him take a few colts for his incoming clients to halter break.

The drive into town was uneventful and Jimmy stopped at Mason's office to inform him of his plans. Mason was a little doubtful of the plan to have the clients halter break young colts, but finally relented and wished Jimmy well.

Driving on to the Wilson Ranch, Jimmy fine-tuned his plan for the clients. He could furnish each youngster with a weaner calf for a 4-H or FFA project. Each youngster would have to care for the calf, halter break him, brush him and get him ready for the county fair. A big part of the plan was to have each youngster show his calf at the fair. The calves would be shown then sold at the fair. The calves generally brought extremely high prices at the sale and most of the youngsters would use the money to go to college. The money that the clients at the ranch got for their calves would present a problem. The youngsters would have to pay for the feed the calves used and their share of the proceeds probably wouldn't be used to further their education. What would they do with it? They would also need to pay the ranch for the calves. This would serve to increase the income of the ranch and help put it on a self-sustaining basis.

Jimmy decided that Mason could go over these details with the youngsters and determine what course of action to take. Part of their rehabilitation program should include some education with regards to handling money.

As he got closer to the Wilson Ranch, Jimmy wondered how he should approach Bud Wilson about getting some weaner colts for the youngsters to halter break. He had to be successful in this aspect of his idea, halter-breaking the colts was a large part of his program to put these youngsters on a successful path.

Jimmy drove into the Wilson Ranch and felt like he was returning home. It still surprised him how much he had become a part of this ranch. He walked into the lodge and found Bud Wilson in his office.

"Jimmy! Jimmy McIntyre!" exclaimed Bud, as he wheeled himself around the desk. "What brings you out to this part of the country, my boy?" Bud didn't give Jimmy a chance to answer. "Sit down and tell me what you've been up to."

Jimmy took Bud's extended hand as he sat down. He didn't take offense at Bud's comment about "my boy." He was at home here and felt a part of the family.

Bud asked, "So how's the Rehabilitation Ranch manager doing?"

"I'm fine," answered Jimmy. "But I wanted to talk to you about the ranch and what we're trying to do."

"Is the ranch in trouble?"

"No more than any other ranch just getting started," answered Jimmy. "We've finally got a bunkhouse built and, frankly, one reason I'm here is that I'm not much help doing the finishing work. There's been a lot of money donated to our project and I don't want to see it fail."

Bud laughed. "There was a lot donated in starting a lot of ranches in the early days. The only problem was that many of the folks doing the donating were unaware that they were donating! So what brings you out here?"

"We're going to have a lot of kids start arriving as soon as the bunkhouse is completed," said Jimmy. "As you know, they're juvenile delinquents. They need something to keep them busy or they'll get in trouble and we won't be doing our job. I thought the Wilson Ranch might let us take some weaner colts and halter break them for you during the winter."

"How many would you need?"

"About ten," answered Jimmy.

"Well," said Bud, "that's a good idea, but, as you know, Honey and Sally are actually managing the ranch now. You'll have to talk to them. They're out on rides now, but they'll be in soon. Put your bedroll in the bunkhouse and plan on staying the night. You'll have plenty of time to talk to them after supper."

Jimmy looked at Bud sheepishly. "I forgot my bedroll."

"Ha!" replied Bud. "Get one of the maids to help you with some sheets and blankets and a pillow. You know where we keep that stuff."

At supper that night, after everyone had returned from their rides, Jimmy got Sally and Honey and explained his idea to them.

"That's a good idea, Jimmy," said Honey. "However, I'd just as soon keep our colts here so I can monitor how they're comin' along. Besides that, we've got our winter help hired an' Pat an' I need somethin' to do durin' the winter. I'm afraid we can't help you out."

Jimmy looked a little crestfallen. He had counted heavily on help from the Wilson Ranch; perhaps too heavily, and now it looked like he wasn't going to get it.

"We might still be able to help," said Sally. "Maybe not with what you wanted, but with an idea."

Jimmy's spirits rose a little. "What's that?"

"Well," answered Sally, "the BLM has been gathering a lot of wild horses and putting them up for adoption. Why don't you approach them with your idea? Perhaps you could even talk them into donating colts for your cause. You know, they're putting a lot of colts in the prisons and letting the inmates break them and then selling them as started colts. Your program might fit in nicely with their program."

"That's an idea," said Jimmy. "I hadn't thought of that. I'll give them a try."

"Now," said Honey, "tell us how your ranch is comin' along."

Jimmy explained how the construction was progressing and admitted he was there because he wasn't much good at the handyman chores.

Honey laughed. "But you're out doin' somethin' that should benefit the ranch. Who knows, you might become a decent ranch manager!" They all laughed.

Jimmy spent the rest of the evening visiting with Bud, Sally, Honey, and Pat and a few of the guests. Some of the guests showed a great deal of interest in Jimmy's Rehabilitation Ranch and Jimmy even had the thought he could turn this visit into a fundraising project. He decided against it, thinking it might be in poor taste.

The next day Jimmy watched as Honey and the rest of the help brought in the saddle horses. He would have liked to help, but wasn't invited—they had plenty of help.

At breakfast, Honey said, "You come by when we have our horse sale next fall. We might have a cull dude horse or two that we could make available to your outfit. No promises, but there could be a possibility there."

"Let me know when it is. I could probably swing it."

Sally got up from the table, went to the office and returned. "Here's a copy of our flyer with our sale dates," she said, handing the flyer to Jimmy. "Of course, they'll be a place for you to stay."

"Make sure you stop in and see your folks when you go to town," said Bud. "They're always asking if we've heard anything from you."

"Yes sir," said Jimmy. "I'll stop and visit with them then go to the BLM office."

The drive back to town was somewhat of a disappointment. Jimmy had failed to get what he wanted from the Wilson Ranch and as he thought about it, his spirits weren't lifted. However, he did have Sally's suggestion and as he thought about how to present the idea to the BLM people, he did see some possibilities. He began to feel better.

He stopped at his parent's house and had a good visit with them and made arrangements to spend the night there. He called the BLM office and made an appointment to see the district manager the next day at eight o'clock.

The next morning he was up at five as was his custom. His folks wouldn't be up until six and he felt lost with nothing to do for an hour. He made himself some coffee and breakfast and decided to make enough for his folks. *Scrambled eggs, some bacon, and pancakes ought to suffice,* he thought, as he prepared the meal.

"Careful you don't burn the cakes!" The voice surprised him. It was his mother.

"I didn't mean to wake you," said Jimmy. "I thought I'd fix you some breakfast."

"That's all right," said his mother, "you sit down, I'll take over from here."

"But I wanted to do you a favor."

"You'd do me a bigger favor by doing what you're told. You've used more dishes, pots and pans than what you need, and you've spilled pancake mix all over, in addition to leaving egg whites on the counter. It'll take me all morning to clean up after you," his mother said, laughing.

Jimmy laughed and sat down with his coffee. As he sipped his coffee, he pondered the best way to present his plan to the BLM.

At seven-thirty, he said goodbye to his folks and went to the BLM office. He was there early and watched as the BLM employees arrived. He wondered who he would be talking to. Just before eight, he went to the front door. It was locked—they hadn't opened yet.

Rather impatiently, he waited for the office to open. At a few minutes after eight, the door was unlocked and Jimmy entered the office.

"May I help you?" The question came from a pretty young lady who appeared to be the receptionist.

"I have an appointment to see the district manager at eight o'clock," answered Jimmy.

"He hasn't arrived yet," said the receptionist. "What was it about? Maybe I can help you."

"It was about getting some wild horses," replied Jimmy.

"I can help you with that," she said. She went to a filing cabinet and got some papers and handed them to Jimmy. "Fill these out and leave them with me. I'll see that they get into the proper hands."

"Apparently you don't understand," said Jimmy, becoming somewhat irritated. "I have an appointment to meet with the district supervisor in person about obtaining some wild horses for a youth rehabilitation program. I need to meet with him in person. That's why I made an appointment." Jimmy stressed the word "appointment."

"Mister Brown hasn't arrived yet," replied the receptionist. "You can wait for him and fill out these papers while you wait. There's a chair over there. Here's a clipboard you can write on."

Jimmy took the papers and clipboard. "Any idea when he'll be in?"

"He generally gets here before nine," answered the young lady.

Jimmy glanced at the clock on the wall. *A quarter after eight,* Jimmy thought. *I have to wait forty-five minutes. This is a heck of a way to run a government. I wonder if the head man in all the government agencies shows up late for work every day.*

Jimmy went to sit down and fill out the papers.

"May I have your name?" the receptionist asked.

"McIntyre, Jimmy McIntyre."

"Oh, yes," said the receptionist. "Here you are, right here at eight o'clock. Mister Brown will see you as soon as he gets in."

Jimmy glanced at the clock again. It was well past eight o'clock. Jimmy decided it would be wise not to show his displeasure at the tardiness of the BLM district manager. After all, he was there seeking a gift.

A little before nine, the district manager showed up and Jimmy was summoned into his office by the receptionist. He'd filled out the papers and felt he was prepared.

Mister Brown rose from behind a cluttered desk to shake Jimmy's hand as Jimmy entered. He looked a little surprised to see that he had an appointment with a black man. "I'm Herman Brown."

"Jimmy McIntyre. I'm with the Juvenile …"

"It says here that you want ten wild weaner colts," interrupted Mister Brown. "What do you intend to do with that many colts?"

"I'm with the Juvenile Ranch Rehabilitation Project," continued Jimmy. "We were hoping …"

"And just what is the Juvenile Ranch Rehabilitation Project?" interrupted Mister Brown again.

"The ranch, as we call it, is a project where we take youngsters already involved in the court system and try to steer them in a different direction than the one they're headed in. If they continue as they have been, they're sure to become involved in a life of crime. We want to reverse this trend by teaching each youngster responsibility. I thought a good way to do this would be to give each youngster a colt to care for and halter break."

"A wild horse for a wild kid!" said Mister Brown.

"These kids aren't wild yet," said Jimmy. "But if something isn't done, and done soon, they may well be."

"This is highly unusual for the BLM," said Brown. "I'll take the matter under consideration."

Sensing the discussion was coming to an end and he hadn't accomplished his goal, Jimmy quickly added, "We don't want the BLM to give us the colts. We want to take them, halter break them, and return them to the BLM. At the BLM auction, these colts should bring a higher price, being halter broken!"

Brown showed more interest. "That's interesting. What do you expect to receive?"

"We don't expect to receive anything," said Jimmy. "The real benefit will come to the youngsters. Of course the BLM will benefit, having halter-broke mustangs to sell."

"Do you have any printed information on your ranch and its purpose?" asked Brown.

"No," answered Jimmy, "but I can have some highly influential people contact you about it."

"Please do," replied Brown. It was the first time Brown had shown any positive signs toward the project.

Knowing the interview was over, and not knowing what he had accomplished, Jimmy left. He decided to go to Mason's office and tell him what had transpired at the BLM office before he went back to the ranch. Mason would certainly be willing to help and perhaps even get Judge Reynolds to help.

At Mason's office, Jimmy explained what had happened with the BLM and indicated he wasn't sure he'd accomplished anything. When he finished explaining what his plan was, Mason said, "We'll see what we can do. According to my schedule, the bunkhouse should be done by the end of this week. Judge Reynolds wants to start recommending juveniles for the program next week. You might have more clients by the end of next week."

"But we don't even have any beds yet!" said Jimmy.

"Ah, yes," said Mason. "That should be handled by the end of this week."

"But what about bedding? We don't have any of that yet, either," said Jimmy.

"That should be coming with the beds. We've actually been doing more around here than what you're aware of. You call me when the plumbing and electrical is complete and the beds arrive.

As soon as you call, I'll tell Judge Reynolds we can start screening youngsters for the program. I'll also see what we can do with the BLM. Wild horses for wild kids," Mason pondered. "That might be an interesting combination."

"With time, one or the other ought to be tamed and with a little luck and maybe some hard work, both ought to be gentled down considerably. I better get back," said Jimmy. "I think you're rushing this a little, so I want to make sure everything is ready. I'll have to send Emily to town for groceries as soon as we know how many kids we're getting."

"Remember, Jimmy, this doesn't have to be perfect," said Mason. "These kids can do a lot to complete what needs to be done. Consider it a part of their rehabilitation. I'll bring a couple of kids out along with Doctor Peterson so you can be a part of the acceptance procedure. You'll have a say in who stays and who doesn't."

"I sure wish we had a few saddle horses to get the kids on," said Jimmy.

"I saw a flyer for a horse sale at the feed store," said Mason. "You might want to take a look at it and consider going."

"What were you doing at the feed store?"

"I went to get you some feed," answered Mason. "The club calves will need a lot of grain and I've set up a line of credit for the ranch."

"I best be heading out," said Jimmy, as he got up to leave. "I'll call you when the plumbing is done."

"Good!" said Mason. "I'm anxious to see this project get underway."

"Mister Mason," said Jimmy, "this project has been underway for quite some time. It's taken time to get what we needed, what with the construction and everything, but it has been underway for quite a while."

"I'm anxious to start seeing some results," said Mason, grinning.

Ready

Jimmy stopped at the feed store and made a note of when the horse sale was and where it was going to be held. It was an open sale, meaning anyone could bring a horse in and have it go through the ring. It wasn't a dispersal sale or a private ranch sale, like the Wilson's had. Jimmy thought that this might be good and perhaps he could pick up a horse or two at a reasonable price. Tack would be sold before the horses and maybe he could get some equipment.

He made a mental note to attend the sale. Maybe Emily and Craig would want to go, it might be the last chance to get some free time away from the ranch before the kids arrived.

On the trip back to the ranch, Jimmy thought more about what he had to do with the youngsters to start their rehabilitation. He couldn't set down a firm program for everyone, all his clients would be different. He would have to set guidelines, yet be flexible to accommodate everyone. He resolved to make an outline of what to have each youngster do, from feeding to cleaning the bathroom to helping Emily with the dishes. There were plenty of chores to be done and everyone would have a chance to do their share.

Jimmy pulled into the ranch with a good idea in mind of how to start. When he got into the house, Emily and Craig were just sitting down to supper.

"Better sit down and get something to eat," said Emily. "I thought you might be back today, so I fixed plenty."

"I've got some notes to make before I forget them. I'll eat as soon as I get them down on paper." Jimmy went into his room and wrote down what he'd decided.

"Did you have a successful trip?" asked Emily, when he returned to the kitchen.

"I don't know yet. I didn't accomplish what I wanted to, but I did the footwork. The results will come if we wait for them, although they may not be what we want them to be. We'll just have to wait and see."

"What is your plan?" asked Emily.

Jimmy realized that he hadn't told Emily or Craig what the plan was with the weaner colts, so he explained it to them. He finished by saying, "It's in Mason's and Judge Reynolds' hands now. How is the finishing up coming on the bunkhouse?"

"Chuck, that is Mister Johnson, told me this morning that the plumbing was complete. The wiring should be done tomorrow and all that remains is to put up the insulation and the inside walls. We're almost in business."

"Almost," replied Jimmy, "but we don't have any beds or bedding."

"The beds are already here," said Emily. "Didn't you see the furniture truck outside? They're in there."

"What about the bedding?"

"It's in the furniture truck."

"This is coming together faster than I expected," said Jimmy. "Mason is anxious to start sending the youngsters out here and so is Judge Reynolds."

"We're almost ready, although we need more groceries," said Emily.

"There's a horse sale this weekend in town," said Jimmy. "I was thinking we might go and see what we can get there. Maybe you want to take your car and get some groceries while Craig and I go to the sale."

"It's been a while since I went to a horse sale," said Emily. "I'd like to go."

"That's settled," said Jimmy. "We'll plan on going to the sale Saturday and you can stock up on groceries."

"Craig, have you got all the chores done?" asked Jimmy.

"Yes sir," replied Craig.

"Do I need to double check your work?"

"You can if you want to, but I think you'll find it unnecessary."

"Okay," replied Jimmy. "I'll look it over in the morning and we'll see how well you've done. I'll look in at the bunkhouse and we'll see how they're coming. You know, you'll be the first resident in the bunkhouse."

"I could move in right now," replied Craig.

"You mean you don't like living here?"

"It's a little cramped," replied Craig.

"It'll be more cramped in the bunkhouse when the youngsters start arriving," said Jimmy. "I expect they'll be about ten youngsters arriving any day after I call Mister Mason."

The next day after breakfast, Jimmy and Craig did the morning chores. Jimmy found that Craig had done a good job while he was gone and he told Craig that. Then they inspected the bunkhouse.

They met Chuck Johnson as they entered the bunkhouse. "We're about done here," said Chuck.

"That's good. Does everything work?"

Chuck gave Jimmy a dirty look. "Sure does. Check it out for yourself."

"I'll do that," said Jimmy, grinning, as he walked around switching light switches on and off. He tried all the faucets in the bathrooms, including the showers. He flushed the toilets. Everything worked.

"You guys have done wonders here," he said.

"We've moved right along," agreed Chuck. "All we have left is to complete putting in the insulation and putting up the paneling. As the guys install the insulation, we follow along putting up the paneling. As soon as the paneling is up, then we're done. We'll probably help the furniture boys bring in the beds and assemble them, then we can go. The furniture boys helped us with the other stuff, so we'll help them."

"The place needs to be cleaned up before you bring in the beds," said Jimmy.

"Certainly," answered Chuck. "The place will be livable before we leave."

"That's good. Mason wants to start sending out kids as soon as he can. I guess Judge Reynolds is pressuring him."

"I expect we'll be done here day after tomorrow," said Chuck.

"That would be Friday," said Jimmy. "That'll be just right. I plan on going to a horse sale Saturday and I'll call Mason on Monday. I guess we'll be ready. I'd like to thank everyone for their work. I'll have Emily fix up a steak supper for everyone Thursday night and thank them then. I might have to send her to town to get steaks tomorrow, but we'll do that. Tell everyone not to plan on leaving until Friday morning."

"That will work," said Chuck. "I'd like to thank you. You've been good to work for. You've left everyone alone to do their job and haven't made any last minute changes. That speeds up the process considerably."

"Thank you," said Jimmy. "The only reason I left you alone is simply because I don't know anything about construction or finishing work. If I tried to help, I'd just get in the way. And, I had some other things to do."

"If that's the case, I'd like to sincerely thank you for your lack of help!" They both laughed.

The following day, Jimmy sent Emily to town to get steaks for supper that night. While she was gone the crew unloaded the beds and assembled them. Jimmy was surprised that there were foot lockers and clothes lockers with the beds. He hadn't given any thought to closet or dresser space.

Emily returned and immediately started preparation for the final supper for the crew. Craig helped her unload the car and prepare supper.

Supper was a success with a lot of joking among the crew. Jimmy gave a little speech about how helpful the crew was and how much he appreciated their work. As a closing note, he added, "Society in general should be grateful to you fellers for your work. With the completion of this bunkhouse, and the admittance of our clients, we should be able to remove a number of juvenile delinquents and potential criminals off the streets."

This comment brought a laugh from the crew and one man

made the remark, "I wish I'd have had this opportunity when I was younger."

The following day, Friday, after Jimmy and Craig did the morning chores, they went to each member of the crew to thank them for their work as they prepared to leave. They were hooking up their trailers as Jimmy thanked them. Some offered some cash to help the project along and Jimmy gratefully accepted it.

When all the workers had left, Jimmy told Emily and Craig, "Take it easy for the rest of the day. I've got some other things to do. This afternoon we'll saddle up and ride over to the Burkhart's and see if they need some help with hauling hay."

With that, Jimmy went to his office. He had an outline of how he wanted to start the youngsters in the program, but now he was concerned with making a detailed long-range outline of what the ranch still needed. He knew the kitchen would need to be remodeled and enlarged, as well as the dining room. He needed more pantry space and would like a walk-in freezer. Larger living quarters for Emily and a larger office space for himself would be nice also. A recreation room where the youngsters could read, relax, or perhaps play ping pong would also be nice.

As far as the outside of the ranch, a new barn would need to be constructed and a hay barn erected. Some modification of the corrals was needed. He concluded that the construction of Rehabilitation Ranch would be an ongoing project and might never be fully completed. Satisfied that he'd covered everything the ranch needed, he turned his attention to his outline of his program for the youngsters.

As he reviewed his plans, he thought about how to adapt the program to each youngster's needs. He knew that he'd have to deal with a lot of anger and defiance from the kids, perhaps some destructive problems such as fights, both physical and verbal. He also knew that the kids would probably have some issues with a lack of self-esteem or no self-worth. The club calves and weaner mustang colts, if he could get them, would do a lot in correcting these problems. Jimmy knew that his job in this area would be to reinforce, in a positive manner, what the animals did. He thought that it would be helpful if he developed the habit of asking for a task to be done rather than telling. He decided to talk to Doctor Peterson about that when he saw him.

Emily called him for the noon meal and he realized he'd spent a lot of time reviewing his plans. After they ate, Jimmy said, "Let's saddle up and ride over to the Burkharts. I need a little saddle time."

On the way over to the Burkharts, Jimmy spent more time reviewing what he'd already reviewed and didn't pay much attention to Emily and Craig. They were talking about the progress that had been made on the ranch and what to expect when the youngsters showed up.

"When do you expect the kids to arrive, Jimmy?" asked Emily.

Jimmy was so involved in his own thoughts that Emily had to ask twice.

"What was that?" Jimmy was startled.

"I asked when the kids are going to arrive," said Emily.

"Well, the bunkhouse is complete. I've got to call Mason on Monday morning and tell him we're ready."

"Does that mean I can move into the bunkhouse?" asked Craig.

"I guess so," replied Jimmy. "I sorta had it figured that you would be the bunkhouse boss when the kids got here."

"What does that mean?"

"That means you'll have to supervise the bunkhouse," answered Jimmy. "Make sure the bathroom is cleaned every morning, everyone's bed is made, and that clothes are properly put away. Just little things like that are done."

"How do I do that?"

"The best way is to lead by example," said Jimmy. "You move into the bunkhouse and in the morning I'll come down and see how you're doing. You'll have to get it right to be a leader."

Jimmy thought he could tell that Craig's demeanor was improving with this added responsibility. He thought it wise to add, "Of course this won't be a permanent job. Everyone will need an opportunity to assume some responsibility. But you can help them to adjust to it."

They rode into Burkhart's yard. Missus Burkhart was in the yard watering some flowers. She greeted the three as they rode up.

"Emily, it's good to see you," said Louise. "I haven't seen you since the cookout. Get down and have some iced tea. And you and Craig can join us," she said to Jimmy.

"I really came to see Mister Burkhart," said Jimmy.

"Richard's out baling hay in the east hayfield. Don't you want some iced tea?"

"No thanks," replied Jimmy.

"How about you, Craig?"

Craig, thinking it might be better to remain with the men, answered, "No thanks."

Jimmy and Craig turned toward the east hayfield to hunt up Burkhart. They found him, stopped, adjusting the knotter on the baler. "What brings you out here?" he asked, wiping his forehead.

"We came to see if we could help you haul your hay. When will you be ready for us?"

"Not until next week sometime. I've still got a lot of work here."

"That will be good," said Jimmy. "The bunkhouse is completed and Craig's moving in tonight. We can expect other kids to start arriving any time."

"There'll be plenty of hay to haul," said Burkhart. "When we get it hauled, I can start on yours."

"Okay," said Jimmy. "I'd planned on going to the horse sale tomorrow, so if we're not needed here, I can still go."

Burkhart thought it strange that Jimmy might alter his plans to accommodate his own needs, but didn't say anything.

They talked about the hay, the weather, and a few other things, then Jimmy said, "We've got to be going. We still have a few things to do back at the ranch."

"How's Emily getting along with the horse?"

"Fine," answered Jimmy. "She rode him over here. I don't think she'll get much of a chance to ride after the kids show up. She'll be pretty busy."

"Don't you be working her too hard. She's a good girl and a

hard worker. If you want, I can send the Missus over to cook when she wants a day off."

Jimmy was surprised at Burkhart's offer, but only said, "I'll let Missus Burkhart and Emily work that out. Give me a holler when you're ready to haul hay. Have a good day."

As Jimmy turned his horse to leave, he heard Burkhart say, "Don't let him work you too hard either, Craig."

"Mister Burkhart," said Craig, "I'm doing my best not to let him work me at all!"

Both Burkhart and Jimmy laughed. Jimmy thought Craig might be loosening up or coming around with his joking. Then he thought, *He is joking, isn't he?* Craig was actually a good worker.

They rode back to the house and found Emily and Missus Burkhart still visiting. Emily got on her horse, said goodbye and they rode off. As they rode, Emily said, "Louise volunteered to cook when I take a day off. Do I get a day off?" Emily asked jokingly.

"That's funny," said Jimmy. "Of course you get a day off. Burkhart also volunteered his wife to do some cooking. I think they've given our little project some thought and would like to see it succeed. We'll figure out when your days off will be and you can call Missus Burkhart to make arrangements. If she can't make it, you'll need to arrange something for supper that I can fix easily."

"If that happens, I'll have something in the crockpot that will be easy," said Emily. "When will you get a day off?"

"I wasn't planning on taking any time off until this project is well underway," said Jimmy. "These kids will need a lot of supervision until they start changing in a positive manner." Changing the subject, Jimmy asked, "Will you be ready to go to the horse sale tomorrow?"

"Yes," answered Emily.

"You can follow us in your car, do your shopping, and then meet us at the sale yards."

"I don't need to take my car," said Emily.

"How come? How will you get the groceries home if we buy a horse or two and some saddles?"

"I made arrangements to have a restaurant supply company deliver what we need each week out to the ranch," said Emily.

"How did you do that?"

"I got Mason to go to the supply company with me and we set it up," said Emily. "I'll call them each Thursday and our groceries will be delivered on Monday."

"How did you get Mason to go for that idea?" asked Jimmy.

"I simply told him my plan and added that there was going to be too much for me to do to go to town once a week and shop for groceries. He agreed."

"Well, you're sure ahead of me there," said Jimmy. "That's good thinking! I wish I'd have thought of it. We can all go to the sale tomorrow."

That night Jimmy counted the cash he had and added it to the balance in his checkbook. He knew he'd have to keep enough back to get groceries. *Not much to go to a horse sale with,* he thought. *But we'll go anyway and see what horses are worth. If they're cheap enough, we might be able to get one and a saddle.*

Jimmy, Emily, and Craig went to the sale. They arrived early and Jimmy looked over every horse that was already there and every horse that arrived after they got there. When he could, he talked to the owners about the horses and why they were being sold. He tried to get as much history as he could about each horse. He took what each owner said about his horse with a little doubt. They were being sold for a reason and Jimmy didn't want to get a horse that was being sold for reasons that he might not be able to control later. He made notes about each horse he was interested in and wrote the horse's sale tag down in a notebook. Satisfied that he had more than enough information on more horses than he could afford, he went into the sale ring where the tack was being stored and carefully inspected the saddles.

Emily and Craig didn't want to look at the tack, so they stayed outside and watched as more horses were brought to the sale yards.

At ten o'clock the sale started and Emily and Craig went to the barn. Jimmy warned them not to be buying anything; he'd do the buying and he didn't want them bidding against him. Jimmy managed to get a few blankets and pads, a few bridles, and some curry combs and brushes. He got more curry combs and brushes than he needed, knowing that they would be useful with the club calves.

They were selling a saddle and Emily commented, "That saddle is selling pretty cheap. Why don't you get it?"

"I looked at that saddle earlier. It's got a busted tree, I don't want it."

When they started selling horses, Jimmy was surprised to see Mister Mason enter the barn. He sent Craig down to get Mason and have him join them.

"What brings a city slicker like you to a horse sale?" asked Jimmy.

"I thought I might find you here," answered Mason. "I also thought it might be a good idea to see what I could learn about horses while I was here. I also have some good news for you."

"I have some good news for you, too," said Jimmy. "The bunkhouse is completed. We can start accepting kids whenever you want. I was going to call you Monday morning."

"I knew that," replied Mason.

"How did you know?"

"Emily told me when we set up the account with the restaurant supply company."

"She's really on top of everything," said Jimmy. "What's your news for me?"

"Judge Reynolds has selected a few youngsters for placement at the ranch. I'm planning on bringing them out next week to meet with you. They will all have their clothes and stuff and, upon your final approval, they'll be prepared to stay."

"Fine," said Jimmy. "We better stop at the hardware store and get some extra pairs of gloves. Burkhart will finish baling hay next week and we're going to help him haul it."

"Good, good!" said Mason. "The other news I have for you is that I deposited some more money in the ranch account. Here's the deposit slip."

Jimmy took the slip and was amazed at the amount that had been deposited.

Mason saw the look of amazement on Jimmy's face and said,

"We have a benefactor who is very interested in this project and seeing it succeed. She wants to remain anonymous."

Jimmy immediately thought of Missus Grundy, but didn't ask any questions. He'd be able to buy a couple of horses with this added income if the price was right.

"The other good news I have …"

"More good news?" questioned Jimmy. "This is just like Christmas in July!"

"The other good news I have," continued Mason, somewhat upset, obviously not used to being interrupted, "is that the judge contacted the BLM and you will be getting eight weaner colts, is that the right term?"

"That's the right term," answered Jimmy. "When?"

"They should be arriving at the ranch next week sometime," replied Mason.

"That's good. We'll be ready for them. It looks like we're making a go of this idea."

"The plan is started," said Mason. "But the results will depend largely on you and how well you can help these kids adapt to a better way of living."

"That's true to a certain degree," said Jimmy. "But the real results will depend upon the kids themselves. Some will succeed and some won't. But we'll do the best we can. The horses will be the ones that will really make the changes. We're ready!"

Other Books by Stu Campbell

Horsing Around a Lot

Horsing Around the Dudes

Humor Around Horses

You Can't Be Serious!

Comedy Around the Corral

More Humor Around Horses

A Young Cowboy's Adventure

Honey

Surprise!

Intruders

Expectations

Frozen

Advice

Broken

Ginny